YESTERDAY, AT THE HOTEL CLARENDON

Yesterday, at the Hotel Clarendon

A NOVEL BY NICOLE BROSSARD

TRANSLATED BY SUSANNE DE LOTBINIÈRE-HARWOOD

COACH HOUSE BOOKS   TORONTO

Originally published in 2001 as *Hier* by Editions Québec Amérique Inc.

This translation was funded by the Canada Council for the Arts Translation Grants program. The publisher would also like to thank, for their support, the Block Grant programs of the Canada Council for the Arts and the Ontario Arts Council. We also acknowledge the Government of Canada through the Book Publishing Industry Development Program.

LIBRARY AND ARCHIVES CANADA CATALOGUING IN PUBLICATION

Brossard, Nicole
[Hier. English]
　　　Yesterday, at the Hotel Clarendon / Nicole Brossard ; translated into English by Susanne de Lotbinière-Harwood.

Translation of: Hier.
ISBN 1-55245-150-x (bound).--ISBN 1-55245-165-8 (pbk.)

　　　I. Lotbinière-Harwood, Susanne de II. Title. III. Title: Hier. English.

PS8503.R7H5313 2005　　　　C843'.54　　　　C2005-900866-0

Nobody can anything about it
but objects but things
nobody nobody
but once upon a time every time
never always and yet
Gaston Miron

The wind must be saved
Alejandra Pizarnik

YESTERDAY

While others march gaily toward madness in order to stay alive in a sterile world, I strive for preservation. I cling to objects, their descriptions, to the memory of landscapes lying fully drawn in the folds of things around me. Every moment requires me, my gaze or sensation. I become attached to objects. I don't readily let go of days by banishing them to the blank book of memory. Certain words ignite me. I take the time to look around. Some mornings, I yield to the full-bodied pleasure of navigating among seconds. I then lose my voice. This doesn't bother me. I take the opportunity to lend an ear to ambient life with an eagerness I never suspected. The idea of remaining calm doesn't displease me. Some days I make sure everything is grey, like in November, or sombre, for I like storms.

It doesn't take much to upset me. I read a lot. I've a sharp eye for misfortune. I rarely talk about misery. I grew up surrounded by the beauty of white winters; every summer for years, I drowned in the unsettling heat of July, buried body and soul in the noble and frivolous green of vegetation lightly tousled by the wind coming off the river. In town, we lived across from a park. Stray seagulls often performed great landing manoeuvres in front of the house before softly, softly wedding their sleek wings to the dawn's fresh dew. This gave me pleasure and I concluded that I was a happy child.

I rarely talk about my little fears. I don't know how to explain a mother's love for her children. I own no weapons, like the folks to the south do. Little nothings don't shake me up. When the ice storm plunged us into the cold, I read four essays on antiquity under the most tragic lighting. I'm easily influenced, and it upsets me to realize I'm at the mercy of a statistic, of a proverb, of three chapters I suspect were written under the force of the tidewaters of violence or of deepest despair.

Yesterday, I walked for a long time. First day of May. People were making their presence felt throughout the city. I folded myself into a group of workers in blue aprons singing with their throats fully open like flags unfurled atop a ship's main mast. After leaving their vocal ensemble I felt lost. I no longer knew where I was. I thought about the wandering children seen in war movies, about their mothers, their crazed eyes when they've just grasped the fact that they will never see them again. I often think about war, but the way one thinks about eating a soda cracker. I mean I quickly forget I've just been thinking about war.

I don't know much about pain but I'm convinced that, in order to write, one must at least once in life have gone through a devastating, an almost agonal energy. I don't much like using the word *agony*. Since Mother's death, I know it means to gasp for breath, the self enclosed in tiny blue veins like butterflies about to fly off far away. Agony: I see it's about the eye, an inward turning of the eye even though the pupil is working very hard to say goodbye, to ask about the weather, to let the light in, ever so little, ever so little.

Words ignite me. This is very recent. Actually, I believe it's since I've been working at the Museum of Civilization, on Dalhousie Street. I've been assigned the job of preparing notices to describe, date and geographically situate the provenance of the objects exhibited. I take notes. I'm the one who composes. I enjoy pronouncing the words out loud as I write them: callipygian statuettes, Celtic brooches, porcelain dolls, antique pistols, ritual knives made of gold. I occasionally accept short contracts with contemporary art galleries in Montréal. Yesterday, for example, it was odd writing *2000* without adding *BC*.

Y*esterday, during the vernissage:* I'm looking around at people. I recognize the astonishment in their eyes due to the simple, almost nonchalant fear leading them unhurriedly from one urn to another. It's hot. Men mop their foreheads. Women pat the top part of their bosoms where the flesh is soft and inviting.

Fabrice Lacoste comes and goes in the large exhibition hall. Smiling, welcoming, he offers advice, information, sometimes a few words, which, instead of enlightening the visitor about the exhibition, make it even more mysterious and thus more desirable. To those enquiring about the location of White Room Number 1, he has a strange way of answering with his hand closed, thumb vertical, index finger pointing in the right direction.

Time glistens in time.

It's been a month already since Simone Lambert gathered the entire staff around the crates that had arrived that day. She talked at length about the exhibition, about its importance and our good fortune in producing it. She went into detail about the little gestures and precautions to be taken, then discussed the strange sense of well-being we would experience once committed to the exhibition. She warned us about the vertigo followed by a certain vulnerability we were sure to feel during the first weeks after the opening of *Centuries So Far*. 'We must be responsible before history, not let it pull us into oblivion.'

It had taken three years of negotiation, four trips to the Middle East, the patience of a saint and a woman's iron will to overcome all the pitfalls and red tape that had come up, cultural misunderstandings and sexist pettiness, border bureaucracy and tricky transportation, to end up on this gorgeous warm spring today. Now time rushes straight at Simone Lambert, straight at her body, her life, her future. It winds around her genes like the serpent around the Tree of Knowledge. Time manufactures time using her skin, her bones, her way of walking, of addressing people who, having noticed her leaning against the rail of the mezzanine, come over to congratulate her.

Down below, Fabrice Lacoste is talking with a handsome, feline, well-read man. One hand in his jacket pocket, the other twirling to the same rhythm as the words issuing from his mouth. He is having a grand time. No doubt he is going to charm the stranger. He knows. Has always known. He does well with any subject; usually he sticks to ecology, nationalism and archaeology. He aims for the heart of the matter, then skirts around it so as to talk about art as long as possible without being interrupted. He usually begins with a historical fact to which he gives inordinate importance in order to segue into a full-fledged argument, allowing him to slot that same fact back into the proper place in the collective memory and, from there, to launch into a vigorous and sensual description of the passion that the sight of the artifacts should elicit in any genuine lover of art and civilization. He talks, smiles. Soon he'll notice that his interlocutor's breathing has accelerated slightly.

Surprising, though, that the same man who has such difficulty breathing in his own culture has the gift of inspiring comfort and excitement in culture-seeking museum guests. Had he not once confided to Simone just how much living here disgusted him? 'Listen, Simone, I love history, but I hate this city.' Simone had turned cold. Nobody working in this museum had the right to talk that way, especially not in her presence. Lacoste would have liked to crumple up his words and toss them in the wastebasket like a bad draft. He had merely added, 'What is this strange passion of ours? Are we interested only in tombs, urns and masks? I know, love what's around you. At least understand it. But aren't we headed for our own demise with all these fragments of mourning haunting us in the name of civilization? We've been living among collections of arrows, crucifixes, rosary beads, ciboria, rocking chairs, for fifteen years. It drives me crazy.'

That day, Lacoste had gone back to his office without closing the door behind him. Simone had overheard him asking his secretary to put him in touch with the director of the Uffizi Galleries, then, lost in thought, Simone turned toward the window. In her head, spring was stirring faraway landscapes that had haunted her since the day of her very first dig. For months everything had been blue as if God existed, then every emotion had become tinged with white, for a sweet forever-lasting folly had gripped the stone-and-bone landscape. For months she'd shared the most precious moments of her life with Alice Dumont. They'd gone from site to site in search of a future and of words that would make of their love a reality.

Since Mother's death, I've started saying what I think to imaginary people. I voice my ill humour, my thoughts, my fears. I also try to imagine the answers when things are cracking up in my mind. Saying everything doesn't necessarily make me happy and, indeed, I don't know why there's such emphasis on all and sundry telling their story, and what's more, doing it live. As of yesterday, it's as if I'd become a better person, sparked by some flame that sets me dreaming in a world where no one dreams of dreaming anymore. Misfortunes multiply like beasts amid technological knowledge. Knowledge spreads like misery. My imagination seems to work too quickly; its volume doubles with the heart's every intention. Without end, the images violently interpenetrate, changeable and indescribable. I go to the theatre often. All forms of dialogue arouse my curiosity. I'd like to understand what gives dialogue its nobility and what makes it a high art for those of us who live wrapped around solitude like harmless boas. What is the value of a question in a dialogue? How important are the answers?

Yesterday, on my way back from the museum: my head is full of images of storms. A boundless sea of paintings and photographs. Other storms I build like a backdrop, with sombre and anonymous characters, impossible to identify. I remain thus all evening, pressed up against the existence of a storm without feeling threatened. Waiting. After a while I become, I am, the storm, the disruption, the precipitation, the agitation that puts reality in peril.

Sitting in front of the big window of her river-view apartment, Simone Lambert is reading the correspondence of Marie de l'Incarnation for the fourth time in twenty years. Every five years she immerses herself in ordinary life as it was lived in New France around this woman who captivates her more than anything. With every rereading she tries to sort out what belongs to the woman, to France, to the seventeenth century, to the random circumstances of a life, such as the freedom this woman recovered barely two years after marrying. Simone Lambert has always enjoyed autobiographies, enjoyed reading the correspondence of the world's great men and of the women who make up its core. She knows that people's worth ably reveals itself through the long-lasting words that can be elicited only by love and friendship. She likes standing silently in the dailiness of women and men who knew how to talk about the wind on their skin, about the fire in their bellies and about every possible storm containing high levels of historical violence.

With every reading she discovers unsuspected landscapes, unknown aspects of Marie Guyart's personality, simple anecdotes that give her a better idea of daily life in the land. She carefully scans for any information likely to justify new digs in the city. Still today, the mere hint of a rumour making plausible the possibility of a new find is all it takes for her to decide to go and probe the streets of the capital. She imagines herself discovering precious objects or mysterious bones overlooked by previous archaeological forays – just as, at the time, while walking along the Seine, Alice liked to fancy that fate would guide her hand to the first edition of a major work or a manuscript thought to be lost forever.

The telephone rings. It's Fabrice. He retells, verbally transcribes, the praise for the exhibition circulating on the Web. All are enthralled with the lion, the Venus of Prussia and the back of the silver mirror in Niche Number 7.

The call has extracted Simone from her bubble of harmony and melancholy. She decides to go and indulge her pleasure and solitude on the Plains of Abraham. From Rue de Bernières it's only a three-minute walk on fresh grass before she reaches the green bench where she often comes to gaze at the great river running to the sea. On the opposite shore, Irving Oil's reservoirs and tall chimney stacks whose smoke always ends up merging with the clouds and their graffiti over Lévis.

For each index card I invent a caption through which I relive part of the life of the object as if my own story depended on it. It's my only way of penetrating the core of the artifact, of spending some time there mentally so as to breathe in the climate of the period attached to it, of entering its landscape with my contemporary sorrow. Yesterday, I hadn't realized its magnitude. No sorrow's ever a waste. On the contrary, it's intensely alive, nourished by ever greater disasters, deliberately fostered, it would appear, to create new industrial waste sites where one and all can dump their grief. Sorrow is constant. Everything around it disappears: parents, friendships, buildings surrounded by the most golden olden days and yesteryears like so many friezes and church squares.

Contemporary sorrow doesn't enter all objects the same way. Some resist grief better than others, be it collective, like that of war, or intimate, like the ache of a broken heart. Collections of radios, cameras and pens are those that most easily absorb the sadness, the nostalgia, the enormity of the sorrow mutely at work, making us die of anxiety when confronted with the obvious fact of the short term.

I don't usually entertain such thoughts. Sorrow flows naturally into the object and the object naturally regains its small-object lustre while I assign it a name, an age, a function. The impression of secrecy, of rarity and of fragility emanating from small objects, even if they were once thousand-bladed weapons that caused death and spread terror, has always fascinated me. They are like roots gorged with sap, pierced through with meaningful arrows, making them akin to the trees of Life and of Knowledge. At the museum, I have the rare privilege of being able to touch them and love them in their every aspect, to detect just the right angle that will enhance them in the dark and in the light.

Yesterday, an eighteenth-century mirror in my hands: the object is smooth, it slides through my fingers and by some miracle I manage to catch it. I hurt myself in doing so. I think about the word *speculum*, about all the centuries assembled in our eye, so curious and enthralled with faraway stars.

It's been raining for two days. *Yesterday* is a word I misuse. Since Mother's death, I use it against the present. I'm hooked on the word *agony*. During my entire adulthood I uttered that word without a clue as to the enormity of the struggle it denotes, just as today I no doubt use the word *war* mistakenly. *Agony*, I often repeat the word when working on my index cards the same way some people catch their breath while gardening. Agony: to persist in wanting to breathe the climate of a period in time that is never quite ours anymore. To steal a few hours, a day, maybe two. The day Mother died, it was so cold that Hydro-Québec wrote about it in their monthly newsletter to brag about their ability to keep us warm despite the severe −21°c cold of that day.

I never think of my mother when she was alive. I only see her in the agony of death or dead but still warm. Sunken cheeks. Mouth open. Eyes closed. A life a whole life gone. A child hooked on the metaphysical time that disrupts what is most unstoppable in us: life, the body, that great wound fated never to heal and with which we must deal.

Writing index cards forces me to keep one foot in reality, which I easily confuse with the need to be well-informed. So, on some workdays I gorge on newspapers and magazines. I feel an obligation to know, an excessive, painful duty of memory that makes me feel like my nose is stuck to death and to simple sad things like accidents, disappearances, unspeakable misery.

Once the objects have been rescued from disappearance, from oblivion, once reinserted into the present and offered up to the gaze of the living, reality circles round them depending on how we preserve and destroy them.

Life has taken on a different meaning since I've been living here. In my little apartment on Rue Racine, I've started experiencing bouts of sadness as though I'd forever lost the enjoyment of caresses and of the great bursts of laughter that accelerate our fall into infinity.

Y*esterday, I had the day off:* after two years of hard work in Québec City, I finally decide to visit the Martello tower and the windmills near Boulevard Langelier. The existence of a Martello tower close to my apartment, combined with the early morning grey, brought back to mind the landscape of Dublin, the joy I experienced during that short trip along the coast from Dublin to Dun Laoghaire.

The bus sped by the Martello tower. I was barely able to make out the sandstone, the rounded erectile grey mass whose perfectly smooth surface offers no breach to the enemy's assault. During that brief moment I repeated *Molly/Martello* to the point of feeling Molly's body against mine. The sweet touch of her breasts on mine. With the tower already far behind, I tried to engage in a conversation with the woman sitting next to me. I immediately felt such linguistic incompetence that I quite naturally withdrew into a mellow silence, thinking, Joyce was resolutely hostile to the use of quotation marks, and especially to their use in dialogue.

I met Carla Carlson at the Hotel Clarendon bar one evening in March. Since then we've been meeting twice a week. Every two years she spends three months in Québec City, four if necessary, to finish a new manuscript. She stays at the Clarendon, asks for a room with a wafer-thin view of the river – the same one for the last ten years. She speaks a beautiful French, and when she laughs it gets even better; her every word changes into a luminous humid landscape. I put a lot of care into preparing for my rendezvous with Carla Carlson. Ever since our first encounter, she has never stopped contradicting me about everything, as though this were a noble and philosophical stance that sharpens our sense of responsibility and conviviality. Putting an argument to death gives her a pleasure she terms erotic. Some evenings she sinks into an inexplicable muteness and always at the most strategic moment of a conversation – that is, when everything finally seems easy, intimate and conducive to a gentle relaxation of words open to metaphysics and to any other proposal that honours life. After all these years of writing she has kept a naïveté that allows her, so she says, to remain at an animal level, where it's easier for her to develop her storytelling talent. 'This is how I excel at naming wild forest animals and others whose juicy, well-seasoned flesh finds its way onto our urban plates.' In the jumble of our conversations, she often talks about her father, about her way of walking around with him as if he were her property. The man could have been a poet born in Swift Current or North Battleford. A tall dishevelled man with Viking ancestors, he was built like a truck driver and looked like a dreamer. Over time he had developed a quintessentially Canadian style. Carla could always see him standing very straight, feet planted on the asphalt of northern highways, his shrewd blue eyes sensing the satin wind, scanning the future, women and the east, which always made him nostalgic, like when we watch time going by and the whiskey going down in our glass. Mythical and unfathomable, this man reappears in all her novels. Like so many women who grew up on the Prairies, Carla has taken possession of her father's soul, meaning that she has lassoed the man like a rowdy character at the back of her memory, has sentenced him to suffer her every writer's whim. She calls him *the old man, Father* or *my papa*, depending on whether pity, duty or affection is pushing her pen, the pen of a woman too young, too old.

Simone Lambert has been living in Québec City for twenty years. She knows the city well, having spent some time there several years earlier. She'd left Montréal following an invitation from the ministry of culture to run the future Museum of Civilization. She'd been given carte blanche, a rather appreciable budget and colleagues both knowledgeable and bold. She'd vowed to give the new museum a worldwide reputation and she'd kept her word, working to the frantic pace of her own wishes and of administrative constraints. With her only daughter living in Latin America she was no longer tied to Montréal, save by a few youthful memories carefully stowed away in her childhood memory box: Saint-Jean-Baptiste Day parades, Santa's downtown arrival, mental pictures in assorted flavours all neatly lined up in the English-language pigeonhole of important feast days: hot dog, hamburger, popsicle, smoked meat, fish 'n' chips and sundaes. Sometimes an old-fashioned horse-drawn carriage drove past her and acted as her collective memory. A snowstorm, a rain of slowflakes over the city, were enough to stir up a mixture of desire and jubilation between her legs. Crystals of reverie.

She'd known for a long time that part of her life would be lived elsewhere – an elsewhere that would make her change-able and lucid. Yes, very early on she'd known she'd have to leave Montréal often, turn toward ancient cities as if having understood that only the remains of the past could ignite in her a vertiginous sense of being alive in the present. Scorching sun and white light, pieces of bronze, bones, fragile pottery, the dust of centuries, gave her wings. Drunk on life, drunk on the beauty of Alice Dumont, she would live as far as the eye could see in uncharted territory, her fascination for disappearing civilizations constantly revived by their inescapable ruins.

This had become obvious to her one day while lunching with her mother and grandmother in the art deco restaurant on Eaton's ninth floor. Every travel story her grandmother told aroused in her countless little joys and questions. So it was that, surrounded by old Anglo ladies chatting enthusiastically, as if they were about to give the vote to French-Canadian women, who still didn't have it, she'd understood that her life would be made up of ceaseless toings and froings that would take her far from her city yet bring her closer to the world of women which, for her, so far remained nameless. Like her grandmother, she would go from city to city, from museum to museum, from mysterious ruin to fabulous site. Masses of marble, panelled brick walls or gold mosaics would speak to her, fill her with joy, for she would know how to decipher the secret which had once given birth to the lions, bulls and winged horses which now and forever had found refuge in the pages of the greatest myths.

And so it was that shortly she would be the one greeting her granddaughter, now a grown woman. Her turn to tell stories and to lay open her world of dreams and work. A few days earlier Axelle had e-mailed, saying she hoped to spend a week in Québec City soon. Ever since, Simone Lambert's whole being was awaiting that encounter with the child she hadn't seen grow up, with the young woman she knew nothing about except that she worked in a big biotechnology lab in Montréal.

In a few weeks, a month at most, Axelle Carnavale would be standing in front of her with her youth, her young woman's vitality, her knowledge and her young researcher's enthusiasm. On the phone the young woman had seemed moved, certainly reserved. She'd said she loved her work. She'd been lucky to find a job after her studies in New York City. She'd been living in Montréal for three years. No, she wasn't married. She would drive up. Most of the time she would be attending meetings at the Université Laval and in the offices of the Genobis company. 'We'll still be able to spend some time together,' she'd added with a little English accent.

The room is poorly lit. A fine rain is falling on the lilac tree in front of the house. A leaden greyness is descending around the cars parked behind the apartment building, the grey of malls and conference centres lost between two highways. Life against a backdrop of Big Macs Shell Harvey's and Pizza Hut. Axelle regrets renting this apartment on Cavendish Boulevard, a short ten-minute drive from the lab. The book she bought in a Côte-des-Neiges bookstore yesterday lies on the sofa. She remembers having started to read it in a crêperie where she stopped an hour before the rave started. She should call Simone. Tell her she has to postpone her visit until next week. Tell her also that she prefers sleeping in a hotel so as to not disturb her, that she may not have as much free time as expected.

Axelle sits at the computer. On the work table, a picture of her mother with a seventies Afro. The photo was taken in Coyoacán, in front of Frida Kahlo's blue house. There is also a photo of her father, who had preferred to be immortalized in front of Trotsky's house just a few blocks away. Axelle hadn't heard from him for a very long time. Lorraine had thought he'd gone back to France in time to make the most of the creative fury of May '68.

I prepare carefully for my meetings with Carla Carlson. I easily memorize every sentence she uses twice. *Yesterday, unusually, we were to meet at the Krieghoff Café:* Carla is seated on a banquette where she can see me arrive, watch what is going on at the bar and gaze into the large mirror covering the far end of the hall, all at the same time. At eye level on the wall to her right, a bad reproduction of a painting entitled *Montmorency Falls*. Always the out-of-control sleigh, the galloping horses, always the smooth and haunting snow. Movement. Turmoil. Just like in the paintings and sculptures of the Americans Russell and Remington, where horses and buffalo twist their necks, buckle their shins, fly like the wind to escape the whip men are preparing to crack with wide and spirited gestures. There, where there are plains and desert, where cold and heat bring things to a standstill, it's necessary to compensate formally with movement which then acts as an aesthetics and a story.

Short hair, a cat's piercing eyes. Black pants and T-shirt. I've barely sat down when she places her hands flat on the table, looks at me: 'So?' Carla speaks softly. Her voice is suspended, flat, even. It's obvious this woman is no longer afraid of anything and that she works with only very few elements of memory. Two or three scenes. Some key sentences. A single landscape. Most probably the horizon. The Prairies. A single season: summer.

Carla rarely smiles. At noon the sun skims the window ledge, coils up the curtains and seeks another ray, starts over somewhere else amid the muted voices. At noon:

– The mind invents with what it sees, has seen, doesn't want to see. I love the novels of Marguerite Duras because she knows how to make pronouns come alive. I'd like you to tell me about the exhibition.

– Just come and see it.

– Urns scare me. Just look at this perfect May blue.

Things happen in intensity. As if nothing made sense except intensity. She uses the words *intensity* and *immensity* the same way. Carla has the power to tell stories from the inside, to map out roads, labyrinths built with sentences she has the skill to turn inside out in spectacular fashion. Then, with a few words drawn from successful comparisons, she projects as though on a screen soundscapes filled with promise.

– Yes, I often detour through childhood as though dawdling there makes the grass greener. I invent crises. I force myself to describe emotions that may not be essential to understanding my torment. It's as if I were trying to thread literature through the eye of a needle and, once I've succeeded, I really believe reality has gone through it. This irritates me and excites me too. Forces me to continue. Have you never wondered why I come to Québec to finish my manuscripts?

– Probably to enjoy a change of scene. I've no idea.

– I come here to make myself continue. To make sure my father's ghost and my mother's story are alive and viable wherever I go.

Mother's silence. It's through the space created by Mother's silence that I view the world, that I learned that another world exists which I could dive into, laugh all I want and exit victorious from any ordeal. I sometimes feel I'm sitting at the back of a large hall patiently waiting for Mother's silence to mould my thoughts. In this place of reverie I also learn to not scream, to not disrupt Mother's silence nor anyone else's.

Just as Carla grew up in her father's wound, I grew up in my mother's silence. And so every time we meet I want to offer her a bit of this silence so she can transform it into a word adventure capable of dissolving the enormity of grief, the age-old mass of bodies and of their fleeting presence by our sides.

Daily living is an achievement. I'm surrounded by cries, by long laments and a wild and shy energy that transforms both the world and my mother's silence into fiction, into an out-growth of life, a nameless virtuality for the souls still asleep at this early hour, who in a few hours will go and stock up on the basics and lose their ability to revolt by hanging around the Galeries Sainte-Foy mall. Without my mother's silence I am left wide open to the static noise that amplifies the coward in each one of us.

Some time ago, while looking for a book in the museum library, I came upon a typewritten page sticking out of a book about diamond cutting. Prompted by curiosity, I read the first lines. I read and reread. Ever since then, this page is always with me. I sometimes read it several times a day. Its meaning varies, depending on whether I read it when I get up in the morning, in the afternoon when the sun floods my work table or when I get back from meeting Carla Carlson. I don't think the page was part of a personal diary. Perhaps of a novel. Some days the meaning of the page seems obvious, on others it wavers like a conversation by the seashore where syllables are drowned out and pronouns merge with the noise of wind and surf. Today I memorized the page. Now it's part of me and can surge into my thoughts at any time. Whole or in parts, slowly infiltrating my everyday life.

She's watching me in the dawn's first light with an intensity that melts me. Her face a vivid world, I no longer know if I exist inside a photograph or if I once existed in the whiteness of the morning in front of this slow-gesturing woman who, never taking her eyes off me, is lying there in front of me, naked more naked than the night, more physical than a whole life spent caressing the beauty of the world. Sustaining her gaze is painful. I imagine, I breathe and imagine her once more. A few centimetres below the manubrium glints a little diamond that seems to stay on her chest by magic. The diamond, no doubt held there by a little ring inserted into the flesh, sparkles like a provocation, an object of light that lies in wait for desire, engulfs the other. I am that other. I am pure emotion lying in wait for the fate crouched inside this woman. The woman offers her desire, sows sentences in me whose syntax is unfamiliar and which I'm unable to follow and pronounce. Words there I cannot clearly distinguish – *breasts*, *gusts*, *ships*, *stext* – and, in between them, the woman's lips move like some life-giving water that cleanses away all clichés, promises that every imprint of the gaze will be sexual, will be repeated and fluid as vivid as the morning light absorbing one's most intimate thoughts. Her arms are open. She opens herself to the embraces that, in mother tongue, suspend reality. The woman has turned her head slightly and her throat astonishes. Her gaze contains traces of that water which, it is said, gushes when memory becomes verb and rekindles desire at the edge of the labia. The woman's gaze sweeps into the future.

Every century stages suffering so that it's always in the foreground of the mind. Thus we can see it transform the humblest gestures into tragedies, brushing aside all life's principles. The world has changed. It changes every day. Simone Lambert was eating a most exquisite sugar pie in the company of Fabrice Lacoste, who was mopping his forehead like during the hottest moments of summer while attempting to convince her that not going to this year's Venice Biennale was a mistake.

– The world has changed. Venice hasn't. Make the most of it. Just think of the *fondamenti* streaming with light, the *vaporetti* letting out a feverish crowd at Arsenale then at Giardini, the *campi* so quiet at dusk. No, really? How about a Bellini at the Danieli?

– I don't have the time. I'm expecting my granddaughter.

– She's twenty-five, I don't think she'll need you.

– Well, I need to see her, to hear her talk about her life and her projects. Maybe about Lorraine. (*description of the dining room*) The world has changed. Reality flickers. Around reality, reality still and again, giving the impression that everything goes on following the quiet rhythm of syntax and seasons. But where does reality lodge? Yes, the world is changing. Life crashes into life. Life cleanses life the way we suck the flesh off a chicken bone until whiteness and fullness are achieved. The world has changed: alienation is back, this time flexible and majestic.

Fabrice was about to swallow a last bit of tarte Tatin. 'How about a little something extra? Why don't I order us each a glass of icewine?'

– If you like.

– You could take the opportunity to go to Rome and see that horrid Cardinal Toffga again. Who knows, you might even be able to come to an agreement about an exchange this time. There's increasing interest in Québec there. The idea for the *Le Québec au Vatican* exhibition is gaining ground. In return, you might be able to get your hands on some of those missals, ossuaries and relics you've been coveting for 2005.

With the word *ossuary* suspended in the aural chain, Simone gazes at Fabrice's hands for a moment. Androgynous and carnal, they close around his silver lighter. A small blue flame rises above his male head. Simone has been contemplating that exhibition for years; not only would it please Québec's old Roman Catholic core but most especially it would attest to the shifting of beliefs, to the plasticity of the convictions and emotions they beget. What did being of one's time mean other than being doomed to doing like everybody else? If need be, to going from one little extra to the next until, having lost sight of reality, maybe even some of its meaning, we manage to weave images and new concepts tightly together so as to transform the real into a translucent backdrop.

Venice. In her mind's eye Simone can see the bar at Hotel Danieli, the Murano glass chandeliers watching over the clients like pink and bluish marvels from a bygone era forever suspended over Alice's tanned shoulders. The world changes. Yet Venice keeps displaying its canals, churches and private hotels. Then the world changes again. Around the corner of a *calle* or on a bridge, young Africans, with their trove of fakewear bags branded Prada, Gucci, Vuitton or Yves Saint Laurent carefully arrayed at their feet on a large square of white cloth, wait patiently to detect in the eyes of tourists the glimmer of greed that will ensure their meagre earnings.

Venice howls in the crazed gaze of the Titian who knows he is being stalked by the plague. Venice howls nobly through each one of its golden lions, howls of silence stifled in the tender flesh of Saint Sebastian. But Simone hears only the water of the laguna lightly lapping on the old stone of centuries, on the suffering that never ebbs from one century to the next.

Most of the major laboratories are located along the highways to the west of Montréal. They often lie between two puny 'resto-bars' tattooed with flashy signs advertising nude dancers. The buildings are rectangular, single-storeyed blocks of cold cement or great panels of tinted glass on which skim fat white clouds like those painted by Magritte and little red cars which at full speed resemble long lean red fishes. The research workers are of both sexes, young, passionate and relatively well-paid. The secretaries are young, touchy and undeniably poorly paid.

At four thirty, Axelle gets into her car. She immediately puts on the CD player. Cassandra Wilson's voice fills the little red Echo, this year's model, just purchased. This morning's weather forecast was for rain later in the day but the sky is still blue. Axelle will make a stop at the Loblaws on Sainte-Croix Boulevard which serves as her drugstore, supermarket and clothing store. Today Ray Something, the tall redhead from Lab24, said he'd made some headway regarding arguments likely to be used for the company's defence in the many lawsuits brought against it. A learned popularizer, Ray Something ends every day by howling with pleasure 'And of course eternity is what I'm getting at.'

Axelle loves her work. She devotes herself to it with a beginner's energy, her curiosity equalled only by her ambition. She spends part of her weekends reading and gathering material about it, the other dancing until, breathless, she leaves the silken skin that covers her from head to toe on the dance floor. There's no controlling her excitement when the music, pumping hands, legs, sexes, even the night's fragrances, seems to want to settle forever inside each and every one of her cells.

In the car Axelle repeats out loud, 'I need no such *pessoa*' (*in Portuguese in the text*), speeding up a bit more each time. Yesterday, in a Côte-des-Neiges bookstore, she'd noticed the word on a book cover. A little later the same word appeared on a sign recommending that no more than six *pessoa*s ride an outdated elevator. Words are grandiose muscles. In social situations, Axelle claims she enjoys reading. She never says that it allows her to stock up on puns that help time go by when she feels like dying.

Now that I'm alone in the world, I'm free to imagine without being afraid of imagining. It's like being naked without a protective *you* as a roof overhead. Facing the night now feels easier, that *buio* of night prior to nights of figs and olives in olden gardens, to acid nights of glass and steel cities, to nights in holy cities where souls frightened by the appearance of their bodies take refuge like swarms of quivering insects.

It's the first time I've experienced the feeling of being without a roof over my head. Nothing between the universe and me. Nobody offering a patch of shoulder and tranquility. From now on I will go bare-headed, exposed to lightning and rain. Head free, head bare. The over-perfect solitude of a woman writing elliptical notices on numbered index cards. Someday, all centuries will end up looking alike under the stars' dust. For now I'm content just to cherish my favourite centuries, beginning with mine, so fierce and sly, brilliantly fuelled by science, unquenchable in its rage against nature. Gradually gobbling up each one of the best ideas that our obsession with comfort will have ripened inside us like little *just-in-cases*.

Adieu, gorgons, griffins, gargoyles and dragons. Nuclear times have dawned, the time of serial killers, clones and bio-industrial pipe dreams. Now is the time of productive sterility and fruitless lucidity.

Simone Lambert looks up toward her office door just as the new employee, whom everybody here calls 'the narrator' because of the stories that even the most insignificant objects inspire in her, knocks twice on the frame of the half-open door. 'Come in.' The new woman puts a pile of small cards on the desk. Her fingers are stained with green ink. Simone asks her what she thinks of the exhibition. The narrator replies that people around her are talking about it, that everything is going well because the exhibition is causing much ink to flow and many cursors to course.

– I'm asking for your opinion, Simone repeats.

– I don't have one. All I can say is that the exhibition creates a strange impression. It acts on the nervous system more than on our thirst for memory, on which our whole sense of history is supposed to draw.

– All exhibitions act on the nervous system, otherwise they'd be of no consequence. Even the dullest exhibition triggers a series of stimuli our nervous systems need to momentarily get us out of the dubious here and now sucking up our quiet lives. Any exhibition snatches us from the present, the better to give it back to us in its agonal fracture.

– By *strange impression,* I mean I don't feel comfortable in this exhibition.

– You need to be more specific; otherwise, how do you expect – ? Thanks for the cards. Please close the door behind you.

Simone turns to the river, an almost Mediterranean blue today. Rare. For in each of its waves the great river glitters an ancient grey, Normandy grey, northern colouring that swiftly engulfs any vague desire for bright colours. The words exchanged with the narrator have upset Simone; and then easily, too easily, she turns her thoughts to the past as if hoping to draw from it new resources that would unburden her of the immediate present.

Delos, 1950. Alice is by her side. In an emerald-green summer dress that contrasts with the whiteness of the stones and sculpted marble. Simone's hands would do anything to make Alice happy. Alice asks for nothing. Her quiet gestures of seduction are directed at the sea. Simone would like to cherish, caress, care for each one of these gestures. And even for their shadows, their origins and their raisons d'être in this world, on this June day when white marble devours the huge perfect blue of the sky. They walk in silence. All around, blades of russet grass throw off little dry sparks which the gaze captures by chance. Alice can't stop marvelling at the Lions' Terrace – lionesses, no doubt, for there's no trace of a mane on the magnificent crouching beasts, ready to spring, jaws wide open on the sea and the world. The island that witnessed the birth of Apollo and Artemis is sacred. The two women tread through the dust and the past. Here and there broken columns, toppled over or rising into the heat of the day like a great mathematical opus tamed by the sun's rays. The silence of civilizations. And always the grass keeps growing.

Y*esterday, still at the Clarendon:* Simone Lambert's name falls between Carla and me for the first time, casting new light on our exchanges. I listen differently. At first Carla notices nothing. Then, too late, realizing that the name *Simone Lambert* is disrupting the ritual that triggers our exchanges, she hastens with an author's cheekiness to pull me close to her father.

– You know, all his life, that man had trouble forgetting. I know. *Je le sais.* Very young I'm able to read his mind, to follow him through the streets of Stockholm. He's looking for his mother. He repeats: 'Flown, gone, *pschitt*! Robbed of what was most precious to her because she refused to laugh and talk like a respectable woman. I was born, okay, but after that. No more children.'

I don't want to enter the fifth chapter of Carla's novel. I want to talk about Simone Lambert, the intransigence with which she requires that the world resemble a museum. I would like Carla to help me understand what's attractive about that woman. Carla speaks and, before I know it, I find myself walking through the streets of Stockholm with her father. It's raining. His clothes are soaked. He's been drinking. He doesn't say anything. He doesn't cry. None of his gestures escape me. We walk past a mannequin shop. He says, 'I'm a dog' (*in Swedish in the text*). He runs his fingers through his hair (*there is no explanation for what he sees*). A car drives by. He turns left, heads into Komhamnstorg Street, enters a little bar next to Engelen's where he orders a beer, is served some herring. He leaves without paying. The owner catches up with him in the street. Because of the fog, both men disappear for a moment. The owner comes back grumbling.

Carla knocks her glass over. I catch it. A few drops of wine spread out on the table. With the back of my hand I clean, I erase. Carla is annoyed: '*What's the matter with you? I need to talk. Listen to me.* Can't you see, my father is miserable. He walks the streets of Stockholm because he's afraid he doesn't exist anymore, because his mother is about to stop existing. Listen to me, I'm telling you a story. As true as my grandmother's life and my father's. Papa, he walks in Gamla Stan. He's unhappy like a man who loves his mother. He knows she will never be able to have more children. He has heard about the law that allows *that*. He knows how *that* is done. I've been working on this chapter for two weeks now and I'm dying inside looking at *your* river, listening to the songs of *your* Diane Dufresne and the poems of *your* Gaston Miron. And that crazy Hubert Aquin you want me to read. He wasn't any unhappier than my old man on chinook nights.

'Papa walks faster, goes down the little stairs of Marten Trotzigs Gränd, runs toward the Baltic Sea. He is still very young. He hasn't slept with a woman yet. He walks with long strides, trembling as he recites a Gunnar Ekelöf poem. Like a crazy man he repeats a word I can't quite recognize and walks in the cold night. He is thinking about Christmas, he is playing with a boat. Under the tree he had just found a wooden boat. All of a sudden it's summer, he thinks he's going to cry because the boat is sinking into the lake. Per and Olaf are watching, so he doesn't cry. The boat resurfaces. Per takes it from him, saying, "It's mine." Papa goes back home. The door creaks. He sits in the rocking chair next to the dining table. Mother is folding diapers. Outside, the Prairies gulp all the wind they can.'

The waiter brings two more glasses of wine. Carla thanks him, then, turning to me as if nothing she's just said existed, asks if we can meet again tomorrow. Without thinking I say, 'Of course, Carla.' Two young musicians are setting up their electronic equipment. Carla looks for her umbrella under the chair. Tomorrow, Montréal awaits me for the signing of a contract with a city-run cultural centre.

Y*esterday, in Fabrice Lacoste's car:*

– You enjoy living in Québec City?

– Yes.

– I'm told you read a lot.

– My work requires it.

– I mean, you like literature?

– Yes, what about you?

– That depends. Proust, Thomas Mann, André Roy. Do you know why *Death of the Virgin*, a painting by Caravaggio, created a scandal in 1601?

– I haven't the faintest idea.

– He'd made the Virgin Mary look like a drowned woman. Her belly was swollen and you could see the flesh of her legs. Plus, her features were apparently those of a famous prostitute. At the time it was forbidden to depict saints with the features of living persons. Today we have no idea how heavily coded art was back then and how risky it was to venture off the beaten path. Four centuries later, knowing how to look at art remains an art. Knowing how to detect a transgression, an anomaly, in a flash, is an integral part of my job, of my enjoyment, I should say. I don't know why I suddenly felt the urge to talk to you about this painting. You've no idea how many paintings have the Virgin's death as their theme. Giotto in 1310, Hugo van der Goes in 1478, Albrecht Dürer in 1510, Nicolas Poussin in 1623, Carlo Maratta in 1686: they all wanted to tell their own version of a story which in principle should be told the same way.

– Where is Caravaggio's painting now?

– At the Louvre. You like women, don't you?

– Yes. You like theatre, don't you?

– Very much, especially Québec drama.

Simone Lambert enjoys walking through the museum during the first days of a new exhibition. She watches tenderly as schoolchildren stream into the museum rooms and old ladysouls proceed with a heavy step, bending over with difficulty to read the notices. Today, children from four schools are expected, and two buses from Vermont. She left the apartment earlier than usual this morning. She spent a long time at Café Krieghoff on Rue Cartier. There she leafed through a recently published photography book about the pyramids. Too late. The memory of Axelle falls across it: her daughter Lorraine is holding the child by the hand. She raises her arm as though waving goodbye or 'You'll never see me again, Mother.' A compact, colourful crowd surrounds them. Members of the military, guardians of the present, of the past and of corruption. Behind the mother and child, a pyramid. Since Alice's death and her daughter's departure, Simone Lambert has managed her life, her desires, her thoughts, in such a way as to keep only an idea of light around Alice and one of silence around Lorraine.

At the museum, she sometimes stops a child on the run to show her a statuette, a mask, an old toy, to explain in two words and a smile what the object's original function was, or to ask if she is enjoying her visit round the museum. But the word *round* unravels in her head and *wound* is what she sees planted mid-sentence. This also happens to her when she says, 'When shall we meet?' and the word *meat* insidiously intrudes between herself and the other person. Today, still, she blushes when dictating to her secretary, 'I look forward to meeting you.'

Today, Simone is happy just to watch the noisy stream of young lives as she spies on their dialogues, the meanings of their words with their high fantasy factor, attentive to the plot line of their little stories which, barely begun, are immediately diverted toward another subject, greater danger, bigger sound, a larger screen. Civilization, culture. Simone goes down to the cafeteria. At the back of the room, some children are wolfing down their sandwiches, a glass of Coke within easy reach. *Civilisation oblige.*

Sometimes I feel like I'm walking on this transparent glass floor where the great humanist principles form a narrow bridge with no safety railing, and it must be crossed while pretending to feel neither fear nor vertigo. Going forward in life, fists clenched, eyes terribly knowing and vibrant with identity. Once we've acknowledged lying and violence as an integral part of the survival and domination kit, once we've understood that the idea of progress is a handy way of eliminating the smell of shit without eliminating the odiousness of pain and death, how can we claim to adequately reflect on the meaning of life? How can what's going so well in my life and what's going so badly in the world coexist before raw consciousness feels like just cancelling the appointment?

People around me talk about the war and frown like professional actors. Yet in our everyday life war has no smell or taste. But it's there, occupying a part of our lives in real time as if time devoted to doing the work of humanism were simultaneously devoted to understanding war. Can one exit humanity without entering fiction? Some talk about war as though it's a scandal. Others as *notta nother choice*. Arguments fray in the course of the conversation. Only television images remain. The non-stop movement of salaried mouths, those of female presenters, journalists, specialists and diplomats. All that's left now is to add up the profits from the next Humanitarian Salon in order to reinvent war as real suspense, a powerful soap that cleanses the tiresome smells of everyday life.

Rue Sainte-Catherine glitters all over, to the west and to the east, storefronts having, they say, regained their glamour. There was a time quite recently when businesses were like cavities on each side of the street. 'Cruising la Catherine,' Lorraine used to call it. Axelle knew only a few of the names that had made the street's reputation: the Montréal Forum, Eaton's, Morgan's, the Casa Loma, the Continental, where, surrounded by young friends and old poets, her parents plotted the revolution and rolled some joints. Today, despite the May sunshine, the street seems forlorn. The sidewalks sag, here and there sad lads hang about or walk around, cigarettes drooping from their lips, dog leashes in hand. Young women garbed in slutty micro-minis and sadness, awkward muscular squeegee kids, boys in big boots and pee-stained pants, all walking around amid suits, ties and polished shoes, walking around like her, distractedly, eyes riveted to something rare, alluring and unreal.

Axelle thinks she should go to the movies, like she used to do so often when she lived with the Moreloses in New York. But the body now needs to keep moving non-stop. Just before the corner of De Bleury, she is sucked into a booming black hole. For a while Axelle wanders through a bank of howling screens and the continuous hum of virtual cars powered by high-cost dreams and electricity. Here and there, young males smoke, jostle each other while emitting sounds like mutants and warriors, rattle dozens of cages to death, just for fun and a rage to live. Dizzied by the noise, she finally stops in front of two timid pinball machines. She slots a loonie into one of them, then her index fingers activate the plastic knobs that allow her to control the game. The silvery beads swirl around in a stream of sparkles until, with a spectacular hip move and the effort of a final answer, Axelle robs chance of two free games. On tippy-toes still tense with excitement, she thinks about her grand-mother who, as Lorraine told it, found guilty pleasure in playing these once-illegal machines which used to be found in snack bars here and there along the road toward the Laurentian lakes north of Montréal. So in the reconstituted taste of French fries, Orange Crush and spruce beer, for a few seconds Axelle imagines Simone as a glamorous character smiling with pleasure in the muggy heat of a Québec summer.

Y*esterday, after signing a contract with the Côte-des-Neiges cultural centre to produce the index cards for their exhibition entitled* Migrants and Gypsies: I stop at Librairie Olivieri. I leaf through some books. In the science section, a young woman who seems rushed turns to ask me if *Genetic Manipulation* has arrived yet. Just a minute earlier I'd noticed that title in a nearby section. With a specialist's flair, I go over and get the book: 'You'll enjoy it, I'm sure.' She thanks me pleasantly like someone practiced in the technique of eye contact. Stirred by her savoir faire and her style, I follow her with my gaze, first to the travel books section then to the cash and the exit.

A few minutes later, a book tucked under my arm, *the body shudders in a slow-motion farewell.* I head for Notre-Dame-des-Neiges Cemetery. My mother's ashes are there somewhere in a little wooden urn. Suddenly the light of the world is unleashed, flowing toward me full of an inopportune silence. At the inter-section of Queen Mary Road and Decelles, a road sign says 'École polytechnique.' The name revives images of terror, a massacre, early winter. I walk between the tall maple trees bordering the alleys. I imagine the body yielding to the rippling pallor of time and its iconoclastic movement. I absorb a simple kind of pain, one without specific object. The pain grazes the vocal cords, the eyes, making all comparisons flawed. I settle into thinking about what the final seconds of a life must be like, the ones they say bear the light of everything that once mattered to the child inside us, those ultimate moments which like greedy gourds fill up to capacity with the energy of the present. I absorb the light. The energy of the present and of its invisible creatures. Around me, weeping willows offer their parasols.

The ashes of both my mother and my father have been deposited in a vault (*description of the vault*) upon which is written a family name completely foreign to our family. GRAVE OF THE O. FRÉCHETTE FAMILY. I'm able to remember the name by thinking about the poet Louis Fréchette. While walking I recall entering the vault only once. It was a spring day when the cold, the humidity and the mud ruined any hope of happiness and the future.

Can gravestones be thought of as ruins? Can they be said to fire the imagination and awaken our knowledge as the necropolises of ancient worlds do?

Is it possible to discuss inner ruins, childhood landscapes degraded by time or learned constructions of the mind, such as stoicism and altruism, eroded by the biting breath of new beliefs? Can one talk of philosophical ruins? I sometimes find myself imagining my contemporaries, arms akimbo, circulating amid ideologies fallen into ruin, finally able to examine them in their most remarkable and sombre aspects. Theories about progress and communication whose finest images so far are the mere carcasses of a lot of small things whose lights have gone out. I also sometimes edge along sites constructed entirely of incomplete images whose broad lines end in the shape of a root or a tailspin, images left stranded like old symbols incapable now of bearing fruit, and about which we don't know what danger or new attraction will have turned off from using them those who originally designed them for the pleasure and intelligence of their world.

I like to be alone to reflect upon these things. Mostly these thoughts come to me when I'm in Montréal and I stream back in time, following the origins of blood and the circumstances of a generation that inherited an impregnable view of the world.

Yesterday, it rained. Highway surface was dangerous serpent. Arrived in Québec at around six p.m., dropped by the apartment to change. Despite my tiredness I went out again to meet Carla Carlson who, dry martini in hand, was waiting for me in the Clarendon bar: clearly, we're happy to see each other. She apologizes for her restlessness, for 'the mad lust of the other me, of the other night, if you prefer.'

– You see, I just had to finish this chapter. Papa often talked about Stockholm, about that night he learned that his mother had become sterile forever. An expressionist night that twists you up with despair. An inky night with a thin shaft of light leading to dawn. Papa loved the early morning light in Stockholm, wan and full of a vibration that transformed his youthful joys into major questions about the Meaning of Life. As for Mother, she only ever had a single story in memory. She told it frequently to my sister and me, to the neighbours, to the pastor and even to the tractor salesman who, I can vouch, never interrupted her despite the twenty minutes Mother's story lasted in its golden-age version, which matches the final version I was treated to for my tenth birthday. A hundred times over, mother went back to the drawing board with the first version of 'The Death of Descartes.' I'm four years old when I hear it for the first time. I'm sitting at her feet, waiting. Mother stiffens, clears her throat, lifts her hand to her forehead as though having to think very hard, then one by one the words escape her mouth like balloons. *Joyous* is the word.

Without my parents' stories, imaginary or not, I probably wouldn't have written. But before writing, I wanted to be an actress like Marceline Desbordes-Valmore. The encounter between the silence of the Prairies and Father's and Mother's wild tales makes me want to scream. However, not only was I taught that screaming is disagreeable to others but also that it's a sign of weakness, so I decided to learn to scream so that it doesn't show, something like a ventriloquist. I scream but nobody knows where the horrible sound, the noisy tumult, originates. I want it to seem easy; above all, it mustn't give the impression of a chasm of melancholy and rebellion one must cross. Three times a week after school, I run to the end of the field behind our house. I modulate my voice with slow, deep, curious *aah!*s that make me look strange, until I feel a round grainy thunder rising inside me and suddenly it all balls up, batters and bitches hard and strong, then it vibrates sudden sudden suddenly like the anxiety of drum-beating with hands and feet in order to attract love. I do this until my artist mouth spews *hush, gosh, rush* and great outcry (*in Swedish in the text*). When the scream is theatrical and undeniably tragic, I term it *humanistest* and stare at the back door of the house. It slams open and Papa comes out with gestures I declare paternal and worried. When it's obvious that through the bushes he has spotted the wisp of a head above the horizon, I know at last that I exist deep in his pupils like his mother existed with her whole being the night of her mad race through Stockholm. I know then that he's no longer worried about me and that his muscles have relaxed. I take advantage of the moment to lasso him up good as I wave to reassure him. Furious, for he knows he's roped in now, it's his turn to caw loudly. Then he goes back to the house with a sprightly step. Alone, I stand in the wind. At that very moment my career as an actress begins. Playing only one part is out of the question. I orchestrate the scene and play several characters. This is where my mother's story enters the picture. I play what I call 'The Death of Descartes.' I am in turn Descartes, which is my favourite role, a pretty young servant who whirls like a dervish, a cardinal whose body is so stiff nothing can move but my eyes, eyelids and mouth. And a parrot.

Her office door is ajar. In the hallway, secretaries and technicians come and go, file folders clamped under arms, cellphones glued to their ears. Seated at her work table, Axelle handwrites a report like she often saw her mother do in their Coyoacán garden. Legs apart, her left hand nonchalantly resting between her thighs; but soon the combined effect of the thighs' muscular roundness and the heat under her palm causes her thoughts to run their course down to her belly. Someone walks by the office and says hello to Axelle, who smiles and keeps writing with one hand while zipping down her fly with the other. The coast clear, her fingers reach under the soft cotton panties, then the index finger goes to work sliding from the majora to the minora labia before stopping here for a while, then there, in lush humidity that would suit the DNA sequences she's been working on for a year. Though technical, the report requires concentration and know-how. Axelle considers getting up to close the door but is stopped by an image: a conch with spacious pink valves set on a window ledge in an apartment likely located in a large city for, all around it, the noise is continuous, thick and alarming. The conch comes alive, vibrates for a moment in the morning light with that little frisson known by oysters when their flesh contracts under the acid effect of lemon. Index finger on her clitoris, Axelle sits still, staring at the fax machine at the other end of the room, which suddenly feels like it's been soundproofed. Time stretches out, then the fax emits a little chirrup immediately followed by a peaceful purring that seems to excite the young woman. A slight tremor. The paper ripples and unwinds its message. The body subsides. In Axelle's head: an ocean sound, then inaudible faraway images. *Estragña*.

51

Evenings when I don't meet Carla Carlson I stay home in the apartment. Nights are tender. I keep the balcony door open. I leaf through my big dictionaries. I consult the encyclopedia for the slightest reason, with an insatiable appetite for ruins and their teachings about our disappearance and the workings of desire in every civilization. Here the Islamic poets Adi ibn Zaid and al-Asha, who were called the poets of the ruins; there the poems of Petrarch weeping over Rome's past, the paintings of Pieter van Laer, of Paul Bril and of Jan Frans van Bloemen, the drawings and etchings of Hubert Robert and of his mentor, Giovanni Paolo Pannini.

I find pleasure in the melancholy landscapes of the vedutists, whose fictional and artificial ruins, displaced in space and time, conceal a fondness for oddities I can't seem to elucidate. Late into the night I work my way back up through time and sometimes make interesting discoveries. Yesterday, I found myself among the Bibiena family, the first-ever set designers for theatre and festivals.

Since I've been living in the shadow of photographs of grief, since Mother's death, I feed on dialogue. I surround myself with ruins as though they were sources of wonderment and astonishment. I don't believe that close acquaintance with ruins is sterile or laughable. On the contrary, I hope to be able to make Simone Lambert an irresistible offer very soon.

It must have been eleven when Axelle entered the great hall of Linoleum, where a rave was scheduled. Twenty or so young people were walking around like smiley lost souls, then without warning started to jump around like badly oiled motors before landing back down to point zero of a conversation, of a series of questions and hiccup-answers swirling in the dark area of desire and intention.

Few chairs, four turntables where a young man with a shaved head works the beat, screwing up his face with every move of his palm. At a nearby control panel another youth works his elbows forward, backward, forward-backward, spurts tons of light down as if to suddenly quench what has now become a real crowd walking upon a raging sea. Axelle takes flight.

Dancing: the only thing that, at the peak of her solitude, could launch her back into the practice of life outside the lab. First there were toes, feet, ankles, calves, knees, thighs, hips, a sex, a belly, a chest, breasts, arms, shoulders, a throat, the open mouth, pink cheeks, the Grecian nose, tender eyes, smooth temples, an intelligent forehead, hair so silky it could have been stroked all night long, then the skull, lower mandible, trachea, shoulder blades, lungs, heart, stomach, liver, pancreas, kidneys, sacrum, femurs, menisci, tibias, metatarsi and the shadow once again the shadow of footsteps till dawn.

She's watching me in the dawn's first light with an intensity that melts me. Her face a vivid world, I no longer know if I exist inside a photograph or if I once existed in the whiteness of the morning in front of this slow-gesturing woman who, never taking her eyes off me, is lying there in front of me, naked more naked than the night, more physical than a whole life spent caressing the beauty of the world. Sustaining her gaze is painful. I imagine, I breathe and imagine her once more. A few centimetres below the manubrium glints a little diamond that seems to stay on her chest by magic. The diamond, no doubt held there by a little ring inserted into the flesh, sparkles like a provocation, an object of light that lies in wait for desire, engulfs the other. I am that other. I am pure emotion lying in wait for the fate crouched inside this woman. The woman offers her desire, sows sentences in me whose syntax is unfamiliar and which I'm unable to follow and pronounce. Words there I cannot clearly distinguish – *breasts*, *gusts*, *ships*, *stext* – and, in between them, the woman's lips move like some life-giving water that cleanses away all clichés, promises that every imprint of the gaze will be sexual, will be repeated and fluid as vivid as the morning light absorbing one's most intimate thoughts. Her arms are open. She opens herself to the embraces that, in mother tongue, suspend reality. The woman has turned her head slightly and her throat astonishes. Her gaze contains traces of that water which, it is said, gushes when memory becomes verb and rekindles desire at the edge of the labia. The woman's gaze sweeps into the future.

Simone sometimes finds herself comparing herself to the woman of action, of business and of spirit, wise to intrigue, that was Marie de l'Incarnation. She's easily moved by the beauty of the river and its shores. Like Marie, she knows how to put out the bonfires of malice and to ignite passions full of consequence. Zero tolerance, however, as regards the stupidity and cruelty that weave the fine fabric of our humanity.

Yesterday, once again, she paused on an event that hadn't captured her attention during previous readings. Since then, images of the 1663 earthquake have made their way into her thoughts: fear knotting the hearts of chests and throats, landslides, waterfalls, animals gone mad, wounded creatures. Then, in a flash, cries and howls shift to Lisbon in 1755, then to Messina in 1783; there the earth quakes endlessly until silence returns, alternating with the sound of Simone Lambert's footsteps in the white cold on Dufferin Terrace. With her is a young woman, a medical student named Alice Dumont. The two women walk arm in arm. Against her arm Simone can feel Alice's chest despite the coat, despite the cold, the wind stinging cheeks and making eyes water so that the river and Lévis are wedged between mist, mistery and mistiness. Alice says, 'No matter where we are in this city, the ground always recedes beneath my feet when I'm by your side. Someday we're going to have to leave.'

The light dims in Simone Lambert's apartment. On the other side of the river, Lévis slowly lights up. The earthquake of February 5, 1663, fades away like a little monkey gambolling about in the ruins of a Greek theatre, an exquisite moment of suspended animation, thinks Simone, when the world reshaping itself forces us to think water, fire, earth and birth. Water, dust, mud. Full-moon evening.

— Strange, says Carla, how my mother, an otherwise very ordinary girl, could for years, and based solely on the comment of a little schoolteacher in Rättvik, have nurtured and kept alive a fictional story about the death of Descartes, a story which to me remains the true story of a gaunt man in a white smock, breathing heavily, coughing violently for seconds that seem like an eternity. The man is ugly, and calling him a philosopher strains the imagination. His thick lips are hedged to the north by a moustache and to the south by a grey-tinged tuft of hairs which the word *goatee* would hardly describe. He looks like a rat whose gene for voracity has been replaced by the one in charge of will. The man's ugliness is touching, for the being gasping for his last breath stirs such questioning and conflicting feelings in us that his mere presence moves and commands our compassion. The dying man's bed is set away from the wall, so the people around him can move behind the patient, watch him or sink into an infinite sadness unbeknownst to the thinker, whose thoughts are already deformed by fever.

Around Descartes, a young woman named Hiljina, whom the man persists in calling Francine. The man's head sinks into a large, finely embroidered pillow which Hiljina constantly fluffs up to its original plumpness. Each of her steps around the bed makes the dark floorboards creak. On a bed table similar to those often seen in paintings of that period, a water jug, wet cloths Hiljina uses to dampen Father's mouth – sorry, Descartes's – as well as his forehead and neck where the very visible jugular vein, now blue like a little snake, at first surprising then so haunting I can't stop staring at it.

In her story, my mother often let speak a voice she said was inner and which she imitated in Swedish. This inner voice could speak only in the name of Hiljina or of Monsieur Descartes. As for the cardinal, he had but a few lines to say and when his turn came, my mother preferred to read a random passage from the Bible. To imitate Mother's voice imitating the cardinal's, I had to pinch my nose and tilt my head skyward. Then out came a rare sound, equivocal and bruised, that made me lose my footing on the prairie south of Saskatoon.

When I read newspapers, I'm careful not to fall into the present of daily life's communal graves. When the shadow of words spreads its disturbing grey over the clueless reports I read in the morning with my coffee, I'm careful to keep my distance from the toxic and rancid beings who undermine history. I prepare my index cards, I strip clocks of large chunks of time. I put the present back in its place in my life the same way we do with embraces in our memory and with artifacts in museums.

What is the present if part of our life consists of imagining ourselves elsewhere, in the past or tomorrow? I don't know if *the present* or *necessity* is how I should name the way we braid our days together so as to allow a vertical escape, either downward with a strong taste of debauchery in our mouths, or upward, an old idea of transcendence ready to torch everything in its path.

Yesterday, I decided to alter the dates in some of the notices. Of course I wouldn't do such things lightly. The dates must remain plausible. In some cases I can add or subtract a century, in others five hundred years will suffice. The closer we get to the present, the narrower my margin of voluntary error becomes. In galleries and artist centres, a ten-year error will appear suspect. Trends, beliefs, fears that last a thousand years, then two hundred, objects that work for forty years or one, media-hyped dramas that graze and criss-cross our lives for six months, two weeks, a weekend. Including Warhol's notorious fifteen minutes of fame, which dumbs everything down: idiots, heroes, killers, victims, the living and the dead. Is it necessary to be as specific with the number of years as with the number of deaths? How many dead does it take for an accident to be terrible? How many dead in an explosion to make thinking turn to panic?

Hard to say if in the long run my 'errors' will have an impact on cultural life and on those of my employers. I was born in 1953, the smells of shepherd's pie and bubble gum smack in the heart of my childhood. Ten years earlier or later would have changed my life. I was born in an urbane city with good jazz.

— What about the parrot?

– Later. Be patient. So, Descartes is a man of few words. Every one of his sentences is solemn. He speaks French. I make Hiljina speak Swedish even though my mother says she's Dutch. As for the cardinal, he speaks Latin. At ten I was aware that this language existed. French-Canadian students had told me about it. They'd even taken me to church: 'Now listen good, he's gonna talk Latin.' I select the cardinal's replies in the pink-pages section of the Larousse dictionary. So, according to my mood, he says, *'Non omnia possumus omnes'* or *'Medice, cura te ipsum'* or *'Non nova sed nove.'* It's more complicated in the novel. I tend to overlay the image of the old priest with Francis Bacon's 1953 portrait of Pope Innocent X. The effect is dreadful – the cardinal becomes Machiavellian. To play the part of Hiljina I nibble a piece of straw, plant my fists on my hips and nod my head while gazing intently at the horizon. Hers is the more difficult of the four parts. I never know what to say. There I am, frozen as if afraid the words will unleash an overpowering anger like Mother's when she gets mad at Father and spews out words. One day I decided to change Descartes's style and make him talk normally because I thought this would make Hiljina more natural, and so this way I could take the opportunity to add my grain of salt about marriage and children. So Descartes speaks slowly, simply, like a tired, happy man. He coughs a bit. I can make him talk like this: 'I loved walking along the Kalverstraat on market days when butchers arrived with their quarters of beef. The din of their carts. There were so many it was like Mardi Gras. You could see the animals' guts. The blood, fat, ribs, nerves, muscles, the pigs' smooth hide. Men call out to each other, bantering. Women shake out cloths over the merchants' heads and the carcasses that are beginning to stink';

or like this: 'I went almost every day to the house of a butcher to see him kill beasts, and from there I had the parts I wanted to anatomize delivered to my lodgings.' Hiljina turns toward the window. The cardinal stares at the wall behind the dying man.

Axelle has just e-mailed Simone. Children are playing in the parking lot. Their screams merge with the computer's electric hum. With the sound of running bathwater. Waterfall. Small of the back. Axelle walks naked around the living room, borne by strong energy operating at navel level and exiting through the mouth in short, choppy phrases peppered with Spanish words. She must have been ten when her mother took her to Cancún on holiday. Leaving Mexico City could do them only good. There would be long walks by the ocean with its shadows, its violets and transparent blues. Shell games. On the beach a little girl is lying in an out-of-the-way corner. Water trickling out of her mouth. Eyes closed. A woman is blowing into her mouth and pressing hard on her chest with her hands crossed one on top of the other. After ten minutes the little girl coughs, spits, chokes endlessly before God and man. She opens her eyes at last. The man and the woman trying to resuscitate her turn her on her side, talk to her, make her say, 'Yes I feel better,' stand up with relief. Onlookers leave. Dazed, Axelle keeps looking at the child who resembles her and who just almost died. She's noticed the purplish lips, a trickle of saliva on the girl's cheek, the body shaking all over. Arms limp at her side. At school Axelle easily memorizes the names of bones, muscles and vital organs. Under the microscope her grandmother sent her, she likes looking at cells embracing, mating like soap bubbles. She wonders if the human body can be compared to a machine. 'This is my body,' she says evenings while walking naked in front of the mirror. 'This is my body. Tomorrow I'll have lost a few cells in the form of dandruff asleep on my pillow.'

About Cancún she recalls the long day spent at Chichén Itzá. Like a moron, the guide repeating *chicken and pizza* to make the tourists laugh. The huge pit living virgins were thrown into as offerings to Kukulcán. No matter that the view is fabulous and the pyramid majestic, Axelle's eyes are glued to the huge man-made crater. The virgins' bodies falling and falling. The priest's hands thrust into a young girl's chest and come out red and shiny, holding the child's still-throbbing heart. The inside of the body is revealed. The body is what we see. The body is not what we think.

Waterfall. Axelle will ask Simone to take her to Montmorency Falls in a week, maybe two. The body, thinks Axelle as she enters her bath, will be the jewel that she and her colleagues will offer to modify in the name of health, aesthetics, reproduction, preservation. The body will adapt to the small commercial pleasures of eternity redux, just as, over the centuries, it has known how to adapt to the violences and deprivations commandeered by fools for God.

This year, the month of May is well-sculpted out of heat, so I sometimes meet Carla at the Martello tower. We always sit on the same isolated bench facing the river. Sometimes we rent a car and drive to Cap Tourmente or Île d'Orléans for a picnic. At other times, shark, boar, pink pepper and island-grown asparagus are transformed into impromptu dining pleasures in an inn.

Depending on whether we're at the Clarendon or outdoors, Carla's way of speaking changes. In front of the river she spaces out her sentences as if to let the wind, the bird songs, the echo of bygone voices blow through them. Never a word about the novel. Once in a while she throws out a sentence like 'Isn't it crazy how nothing really unfortunate is happening in our lives?' Sometimes I dare ask a question, hoping it will bring us back to discussing the novel.

– Did you know that Descartes's body was interred in the 'cemetery for children deceased before baptism or before the age of reason'?

– Yes. Did you know his remains are in Saint-Germain-des-Prés church in Paris?

– No.

– By the way, what's the name of the little cemetery on Rue Saint-Jean?

– You mean the park next to the Ballon Rouge?

– No, the cemetery next to the Anglican church.

– It's a park now. Saint Matthew's, same as the church. On Sundays, in summer, children play among the gravestones.

– Yesterday, somebody told me an incredible story about Jean Cocteau's parrot.

– Cocteau had a parrot?

– So they say.

Since early today, the museum has been the scene of the comings and goings of artists, caterers and technicians. Tonight the entrance hall will welcome two hundred guests for the launch of a human-rights campaign. Politicians have been invited, as have businesspeople, some academics and, obviously, reporters.

In her office, Simone has just read Axelle's message. Disappointment darkens her face like a morning shadow. By the window, the light is acting crazy on the furniture because of the wind through the leaves.

– She's playing games, for sure. You can't be expected to be on stand-by for her, says Fabrice. No way, not with all the work we've got coming up. You really should go to Italy. Three days in Venice, three in Rome to negotiate with Cardinal Toffga, and back in time for the exhibition: *Talking Spoons and Fork Lore*. As for me, I'll go through Leipzig and Weimar. Sketches, notebooks and travel manuscripts: you'll have them all, I promise, then I'll meet up with you in Rome for the negotiations. What do you say?

Simone looks closely at Fabrice, smiles, asks if the prime minister's presence has been confirmed for tonight. Simone thinks about Lorraine, who never knew how to talk about politicians and policemen except by using animal or vegetable names or an impressive lexicon of swear words. Times were changing. Politicians had less and less power. In twenty years they'd have even less. The world is changing. Nothing better than a museum to demonstrate this. And a pool of curators to count on.

Y*esterday, we looked for and found Gabrielle Roy's house in Petite-Rivière-Saint-François.* The house is temporarily occupied by a young novelist. Carla asks her a few questions and says she comes from Saskatchewan, also known as the Land of Living Skies because of its storms, so fascinating they sometimes disturb some people's minds to the point of causing them to break off from their families. Carla's words seem to interest the young woman and, after a short while, she invites us in for a drink. (*description of the living room*) The novelist is surprised that Carla, who writes in English, has come to Québec City to finish her four novels. Carla replies that she's been reading Marie de l'Incarnation, Anne Hébert and Alain Grandbois for ages, as well as some gorgeous books by a poet from the Québec City area who writes about birds. Then they discuss the single life and World War II. The young woman's father was a career army man. One of her uncles was fiercely against the draft. The two men almost killed one another. Family drama for family drama, Carla talks about the adoption, in 1935, of a Swedish law that forced people with a hereditary illness to be sterilized. The afternoon is passing. One after the other, the novelists toss lucky dice at each other, drop names pell-mell into the gathering dusk, names that please: Greta Garbo, Anne Hébert, Ingmar Bergman, Alain Grandbois, Selma Lagerlöf, Paul-Émile Borduas, Pär Lagerkvist, *Anne Trister, Fanny and Alexander*. As each one attempts to instruct the other about her culture and the inner fire that sustains it, I draw Carla's attention to the fact that she could mention a few Canadian authors. *Logique oblige.* Nothing doing, they continue their conversation as if they'd always known each other, as if I didn't exist. I'm not offended. I use the time to observe Carla's face. When Mother died, I knew every feature of her face by heart. It's crazy how we never look at faces when we're speaking with people. As if, from not looking into the eyes too much or seeming not to want to insert ourselves into the other's thoughts, we end up seeing nothing. Mother couldn't defend herself. Her whole face was vulnerable to my worried gaze discovering the curve of her nose, of her eyebrows, eyelashes so short, wrinkles not as deep as I'd thought.

Carla has the feverish beauty and intelligence of a woman forever on the lookout, for whom people and words are due much attention. If she could she'd recycle each one of the lives around her to spare them the consequences of their errors and inexperience. She's in exceptional form today, as though excited by the young novelist originally from Lac Saint-Jean, a region of Québec Carla doesn't know and which piques her curiosity to the point of indiscretion. Before we leave, the novelist shows us a copy of the first edition of *The Tin Flute*. Carla leafs through it carefully as if she were going to find hundred-dollar bills tucked between the pages or intimate little notes once used as bookmarks. On the way back, Carla says nothing. Musing. Elsewhere.

—Descartes is sitting on his bed. He speaks softly. Every word he utters is perfectly audible in the half-light. He's not yet delirious. This will come. Later on, between three thirty and three forty-five. At four, it will all be over. It's cold in the room. Yesterday it snowed non-stop. A light little snow that slants across the eye and is enough of a distraction to impress it with tender whiteness. Yesterday Descartes watched this snow fall, first from behind the window, then the flakes began to whirl above his bed. He shivers. He's unable to keep his eyelids open longer than thirty seconds at a time. So he yields to the freshness of each snowflake upon his face. A little cold pinching, then his skin feels the transformation of the frosty crystals into water drops. Now he's speaking to a woman named Francine. He also calls her *my child, my precious, my little Frantsintze*. Stretched out on my back in the field, I too prefer pronouncing it *Frantsintze*. The effect is better, I think. The syllables vibrate better in the fresh autumn air. 'Frantsintze, bring me some water' (*in Swedish in the text*). Then the words thicken in my mouth and Mother's Descartes says, '*Jag förstar inte*. Why did you leave us so young, your mother and I? Just when you become my daughter, when I finally recognize you as my little girl, God claims you.' At that very moment I always bring in the cardinal: *sustine et abstine*.

Not moving when I make the cardinal speak is what's most difficult. Even when I play the part in full sunlight. Not moving is synonymous with half-light, with being deprived of light. Papa always said that living in the half-light is natural for Swedes; they're used to night even though they enjoy daylight almost continuously in the summertime. In my novel, every time the cardinal speaks he conjures up the image of that portrait of Pope Innocent X I told you about the other day.

Bacon was inspired by a Velázquez painting from 1650. The mouth especially causes me anxiety. A deformed mouth. A careful mutilation of the meaning of life. That mouth haunts me. Mouth of a woman who has had one eye gouged out.

Carla's novel is taking up more and more space between us, estranging us. Bringing us closer. As if fiction were acting like a tampon, absorbing Mother's silence, her father's wound and her mother's invented story. What started off as the innocent pleasure of the spoken word has, through our repeated encounters, become an attraction, an erotico-semantic gap we hasten to fill up with the next conversation using easy reference points such as the bed, the window or the pillow upon which Descartes's head rests. Our every encounter disturbs the meaning of Carla's novel. Refreshing it without her awareness. Even here in the bar at the Clarendon, in what Carla calls the mystery of a city that gives insight into the continent, her novel rips us out of history, out of the quiet temporality of bell towers and convents.

Yesterday, she asked if I'd like to read a few pages of her manuscript. I refused. She insisted, saying she was doing this so that I would think of her more often. So that a healthy confusion would take hold of me, so that I'd hesitate between her face and the face of the little actress lying in the grass in Saskatchewan. She'd like me to share some of her fears and panic, fantasies where America falls apart and recovers in the eyes of a Prairie girl who thinks she's René Descartes and who, because of this mirror, is learning French, hoping to lose that quintessentially Canadian style that doesn't match her aspirations.

Who am I to judge Carla or the naïveté making her write yet another novel? Who am I to find it not terribly clever to have to resort to such a tiny thread of life as childhood *lookit lookit that's me over there!* I always feel like saying to her: 'What do you think your mother feels when she talks about Rättvik, when Queen Christina's face merges with the face of the village women? Come on, what do you see when the clouds sail over your father staggering in the middle of the highway? What do you think about when you go back up to your room after one of our conversations? Do you sometimes want to make room for me in your novel?'

She's watching me in the dawn's first light with an intensity that melts me. Her face a vivid world, I no longer know if I exist inside a photograph or if I once existed in the whiteness of the morning in front of this slow-gesturing woman who, never taking her eyes off me, is lying there in front of me, naked more naked than the night, more physical than a whole life spent caressing the beauty of the world. Sustaining her gaze is painful. I imagine, I breathe and imagine her once more. A few centimetres below the manubrium glints a little diamond that seems to stay on her chest by magic. The diamond, no doubt held there by a little ring inserted into the flesh, sparkles like a provocation, an object of light that lies in wait for desire, engulfs the other. I am that other. I am pure emotion lying in wait for the fate crouched inside this woman. The woman offers her desire, sows sentences in me whose syntax is unfamiliar and which I'm unable to follow and pronounce. Words there I cannot clearly distinguish – *breasts*, *gusts*, *ships*, *stext* – and, in between them, the woman's lips move like some life-giving water that cleanses away all clichés, promises that every imprint of the gaze will be sexual, will be repeated and fluid as vivid as the morning light absorbing one's most intimate thoughts. Her arms are open. She opens herself to the embraces that, in mother tongue, suspend reality. The woman has turned her head slightly and her throat astonishes. Her gaze contains traces of that water which, it is said, gushes when memory becomes verb and rekindles desire at the edge of the labia. The woman's gaze sweeps into the future.

Everything real eats at me. Even though I put a lot of energy into lapping up my contradictions, inhabiting life and its opposite exhausts me. All around me, everyone is talking about their world view. Giving one's opinion is a widespread activity that reinforces the idea that life is a big show where good and evil meet while pretending not to recognize each other. The other day, I asked Carla if lucidity had a practical application in everyday life or if it suited only certain moments of existence. Also, if it could be cultivated or if it was something innate that couldn't be discarded, that stuck to the skin, to the cornea, even to words that help us exist in the vast landscape of emotions and of the idea we have of suffering, of good and evil, of lies.

When I was a university student, I thought lucidity was the most precious thing for anyone who claimed to take responsibility for their life and who chose to intervene in civic affairs in the name of justice and respect for all. Back then, lucidity meant the desire to do the right thing based on a certain quantity of information that, once analyzed, made it possible to judge politicians and the laws they often foist upon the population. Being lucid didn't grant the right to mock those who weren't. Being lucid meant having evidence in hand with which to fight oppression and alienation. Lucidity being an instrument of liberation, it was normal to want to share it with all the men and women who could benefit. Today many of us claim we're lucid, that we can correctly evaluate good and evil, yet nothing results from this mass of side-by-side consciences, for each one is flanked by an impeccable solitude and a taking-care-of-number-one that always seems to ensue from mitigating circumstances. Today, only one part of the soul moves us, ignorant and smiling, a tiny part of the soul we wear like a hip-slung revolver and quick-draw in the name of our horizonless individualism.

*M*asturbation *(1580 – Montaigne). From Latin.* Manu *(hand) et* stupratio *(act of soiling): practice of provoking sexual pleasure (by manual excitation/stimulation of the genitals).*

Yesterday, on her way home from an evening with four women – two secretaries, a chemist and a lawyer – Axelle got lost between Sainte-Anne-de-Bellevue and Île Bizard. To her great surprise, she found herself on a country road, then on the unpaved streets of a residential site under construction where she circled around for ten minutes before spotting the feeble lighting of the highway. She drove fast for a bit until another car sped by dangerously. The car went on, its headlights disappearing in the dark. Against all common sense, Axelle Carnavale pulled her car over onto the service ramp, turned the headlights off, locked her doors, pulled up her skirt and thought of the little pink edition of *Thérèse and Isabelle*.

The book is lying on a stack of files her mother has forbidden her to touch. To touch is to displace and then it's hard to find things again. Tonight, Lorraine is participating in *una mesa rotonda* along with a sociologist, a librarian from Coyoacán and a novelist who has just published an essay on Sor Juana Inés de la Cruz. It's hot. Axelle is home alone. She wanders about aimlessly in the living room. An awkward gesture and Violette Leduc's book falls among the files: 'I detached myself from my skeleton and floated away on my dust. The pleasure was rigid at first, difficult to sustain. The visit began in one foot, pursuing its course through flesh now candid once again. We had forgotten our fingers back in the old world, we were gaping with light, invaded by a rending bliss. Our legs mangled with delight, our entrails flooded with illumination … ' It's a little pink book about nineteen centimetres tall by ten centimetres wide. The pages have been cut with care. Nothing torn, as is often the case when we want to proceed too quickly.

Axelle pauses on certain words. A lot of body. Something alive that operates slyly to project the body into a better, more carnal world. Standing in the middle of the room, Axelle promises herself to become a flesh-and-blood woman and to teach herself at length and methodically about the body.

DESCARTES: After your death, the idea of the sea and the plain never left me. I did everything I could to settle down in villages close to the sea. I was happy in the flat land and, though my sorrow was deep, I continued working.

THE PARROT: Med'tation, med'tation.

DESCARTES: I don't know what became of your mother. She seemed inconsolable, fragile. She started losing her beautiful hair which I so loved to stroke.

HILJINA: You chased me away then you simply forgot about me. I know that your father's death only months after our daughter Francine died was painful for you. Foregoing all sense of propriety, you allowed yourself to weep like a woman. I know you suffered, but there was no need to throw me out like some domestic animal.

THE PARROT: Animax-machine, animale-machismo, anima-malady.

THE CARDINAL: *Intelligenti pauca.*

HILJINA: Oh, shut up! You inquisitive shit.

DESCARTES: Helen, I beg you, let's strive for harmony here. When Queen Christina asked me to write a poem for a ballet to honour the peace in Westphalia, I didn't hesitate to pledge my full co-operation and to put my every energy at her service while promoting the wisdom of Pallas. (*turning toward Hiljina with difficulty and suddenly mistaking her for Francine*) As a child, you were very easily entertained. As a child I needed boats, swords and the wind, but like you, I also loved playing with nothing, negate, rhyme, mime, drown my sorrow in words and Mother's hair. Francine, I would have loved to do with you what I've been doing with Queen Christina for a month. At five in the morning, by candlelight, sometimes while watching the snow accumulate in the shape of a camel's back under my window, I would have told you about the passions that govern us and the phenomena that, although they're simple, drag us unawares into labyrinths we then have difficulty getting out of with dignity. Thus the appearance of a disturbing yet simple passion in our lives provokes the just-right landscape of harmony.

Without any hesitation, Simone Lambert heads for the *embarcadero,* where boats shuttle back and forth between Marco Polo Airport and Piazza San Marco. An hour and forty minutes of pleasurable settling into a tropical languor, eyes glazed by jet lag and madly bedazzled by the sea's glaring sunlight. At first the shuttle moves fast, like on a country road, through a corridor free of algae and high grasses. On either side, people are digging for clams, bent over like in a Millet painting. At Murano and at the Lido, passengers embark, disembark; the sea widens, ceaselessly travelled to and fro starboard and portside by cruise ships and *motoscafi.* The sun shines bright. Strong heat blurs the horizon until, emerging from the water like a mirage, La Serenissima reveals its most unexpected shapes: the campanile, the domes of La Salute and of San Giorgio Maggiore. And travel-weariness evaporates. Time unrolls its carpet between the sea and a vague idea of the immensity which dreams so easily transform into surfaces, flexible, capable of renewing customs and embellishing stories. La Serenissima quickens everything. Centuries fly by. Before the boat docks, Simone will have walked elbow to elbow with Renaissance artists and scholars. Flouting the life sentence weighing on her sex, she will have demonstrated cleverness during each one of her imaginary exchanges with merchants, military men and men of God.

Campo Santa Maria Formosa, siesta time. The piazza is quiet. The heat intense. Next door to the Scandinavia Hotel, the Orologio Bar is open. Simone goes in and orders an espresso. The owner recognizes her. She's happy to see her again. Part of the pleasure of living rests on the joy others demonstrate when they see us again, thinks Simone. It's simple and it works. The multicoloured strips of plastic hanging from the door frame remind her of Monica Vitti in *L'Avventura*. Simone knows it's easy to be afraid that everything is too perfect. Easy to make much ado about nothing, hoping every instant will be chock full, entirely devoted to understanding life better and enjoying it to the fullest. Fine. She downs her coffee, walks the few metres to the hotel. At the desk she fills out a blue form, asks to be woken up in two hours.

Axelle drops the postcard postmarked Venice on her desk: a winged lion on a starry blue background, plus Saint Theodora's column and Saint Mark's with its three-ton lion. On the back of the card, a date, three lines, a signature in mauve ink. The first and second sentences are printed and in quotes: 'Thus we walked from bridge to bridge, talking of things … Love of my native place bestirred me.' Above the signature, 'See you soon. Love.' The stamp, no doubt chosen intentionally, represents a manuscript page from Antonio Gramsci's *Quaderni del carcere*.

As a child, Axelle was fascinated with lions. Seated in front of the television, she would watch their every muscle, and when the image was in slow motion, she'd penetrate their gaze as if it were a door opening onto a world that, provided with the proper vocabulary, she would instinctively have declared horribly fierce and nostalgic. In plush or in plastic, the king of the jungle was an ally to her, a likeable grouch. Her mother had swiftly turned her away from such a notion by telling her about the mercenary lions who used to ferociously attack early Christians. As for her father, he had advised her to stay away from the lions made of stone and of bronze, of marble and of granite, that stood watch at the entrance of banks, museums and train stations in the name of the British Empire, which held sway over the heart of Montréal. Gradually the marble lions had made way for Metro-Goldwyn-Mayer's roaring feline, then for the designer logo lions at Peugeot and the Royal Bank. Still today, it's with a very peculiar emotion that Axelle recalls Patience and Fortitude nobly posing outside the New York Public Library.

A last glance at the postcard. Peter Workhard appears in the door. He's about to come in when his cellphone calls him to order. With a shrug and a wince, he gestures goodbye. Axelle wonders who authored the quotation, thinks that searching for the answer is like looking for a needle in a haystack. And who knows, it may not be a quotation after all but simply an appropriate thought that crossed Simone's mind and which she chose to highlight by putting it in quotation marks.

With Simone Lambert away for a week, I experience an unspeakable ennui while circulating through the rooms of the museum and the corridors of Maison Estèbe. I cancelled two rendezvous with Carla, as though there were some connection between being deprived of Simone's presence and enjoying conversation with Carla Carlson, novelist. It's been raining for two days. The grass in front of the parliament building is a tropical green that makes you want to be elsewhere and to read unusual books. Despite the rain I prefer to walk home. Apart from the museum people, I see no one except two seriously tattooed women I talk with at Taverne Dion before going back to the apartment. I reread my notes on artificial ruins. I'm thinking of adding a series of photographs taken in Chernobyl and Minsk and along the Pripet – photographs of factories and trains decaying in huge fields fertilized by death. Also pictures of ships and destroyers abandoned to rust, salt and their own secretions. Barrels of dioxin, radioactive matter. Contemporary ruins are slow-moving monsters yet ferocious nonetheless. Ruins strewn like fresh waste matter that acts like a wound by reminding us that, well beyond *tempus fugit*, abandonment is a desertion of the senses. Contemporary ruins are to our thoughts what corrosion is to raw materials; they deposit in us images of abandonment that forever contaminate our sense of duration. Abandoned children. Abandoned novels. Contemporary ruins are very useful for fuelling our contradictions. They are in no way useful to art, and yet I am no doubt going to use them to convince Simone Lambert to let me curate an exhibition I plan to entitle *Ruins: Time's Remains, Desire's Reign*.

The *vaporetto* is crammed with art lovers, gallery owners, critics, artists. Few people get off at Arsenale. At Giardini, passengers rush to the gardens and onto the little pebble paths leading to the Biennale and its pavilions. Simone heads straight for the Canadian pavilion, has a glass of *prosecco* while chatting with the artist chosen to represent that country. After two drinks she decides to go and say hello to her friends in the French, British and German pavilions located near the Canadian one. The smell of fresh paint from the installations mixed with the wind-borne dust from the paths creates a strange kinesthetic cocktail which, now mixing in with tired-ness from the trip, prompts Simone to let go into a nameless relaxation. In Venice, but especially in this contemporary place of celebration, Simone feels supremely free, at the peak of her sensitivity. Here, she once again becomes Alice Dumont's lover, a passionate woman whose body vibrates at the slightest contact, even the wind on the nape of her neck. After all these years the images still come flooding, numerous, vague here, well-defined in the more sensitive areas of memory.

Without realizing it, Simone moves with gestures round and full of finesse, not bothered by the snobs and amateurs around her. She can, in this precise moment of well-being, handle anything: sleazy looks, crooked smiles, limp hands, elephant-like embraces. So soars her enthusiasm until, a few metres away, a man stands out from the crowd, dressed in black, hair tied back in a ponytail, shoulders wide. The man has aged but kept a counterculture look, a Marxist hooked-on-history look. This is the last person to have been seen with Lorraine before she disappeared. Standing with a glass of wine in his hand, the man walks into some red powder spread on the floor of the American pavilion, where Ann Hamilton is showing her most recent installation. Something smoke-like made of the same powder hisses from the ceiling like gas and trickles down the white walls in thin scarlet rivulets. On the floor, the horrid stuff sticks to soles and reddens visitors' steps.

There was a time when their readings criss-crossed like tango steps. Simone read certain books just to be able to recommend them to her daughter. As for Lorraine, she read authors she called innocent for the sheer pleasure of discussing them with her mother. Later on they resumed this game, this time by visiting museums and galleries. Simone would propose grand major works, Lorraine promoted young artists whose work and interventions spit fire. One spoke of inspiration and talent, the other of courage and lucidity. This strategy lasted happily for a while, until the day Lorraine left home without explanation and moved into a loft in Old Montréal. Simone was purchasing art for a multinational back then. She was devastated by the feelings of abandonment and rejection Lorraine's estrangement sparked. She invented opportunities to see her, pretending to need her opinion about this or that young artist. She invited her to vernissages where alcohol and projects flowed. Everywhere there were halls, rooms, buildings to be inaugurated in a Montréal being torn down and rebuilt, lips lapping Scotch for some, hands waving placards for others. Lorraine introduced her to Alexandre Carnavale, a talkative young Marxist-Leninist painter. Nine months later a daughter was born, whom they named Axelle in honour of the Swedish figure skater Axel Paulsen, thinking about the axis of revolution that slumbers in every newborn, even a girl.

I'm gradually slipping into a vertigo which, for some reason, keeps me at a distance from Carla's novel. For a long time I believed it was good to let fiction into one's life. That this would make it possible to reframe existence, to unfurl landscapes so stunning that afterwards one couldn't help but love the most ordinary gestures and objects, for, once fiction had traversed them with its kaleidoscopic brilliance, everything comprising reality would shine with a thousand intriguing fires. Fiction was my foothold for touching light. I knew how to make it enter my life like others allow sex, violence or gastronomy into their thoughts. Truth be told, I exaggerate the importance of fiction because I'm quite naturally able to sort out the emotions, words and sensations that emphasize the duty of existence. It's like rolling out a carpet under the eyes of a blind person. While the blind person makes do with the muted sound of the wool on the ground, I take possession of every movement of his face. I enter what blinds him, without losing track of the carpet and its diamond-point motif, always redder than blood. Sometimes I can hear the sound children's fingers make on the warp and weft of looms.

Today I simplify everything, I say, 'Oh, there are no mauve clouds,' and in just a few thoughts I travel around the world like Simone tours civilization, forced to handle bones and weapons throughout an entire project. Sometimes while listening to Carla I feel like kissing her on the mouth. Like moulding my lips to the words she pronounces.

She's watching me in the dawn's first light with an intensity that melts me. Her face a vivid world, I no longer know if I exist inside a photograph or if I once existed in the whiteness of the morning in front of this slow-gesturing woman who, never taking her eyes off me, is lying there in front of me, naked more naked than the night, more physical than a whole life spent caressing the beauty of the world. Sustaining her gaze is painful. I imagine, I breathe and imagine her once more. A few centimetres below the manubrium glints a little diamond that seems to stay on her chest by magic. The diamond, no doubt held there by a little ring inserted into the flesh, sparkles like a provocation, an object of light that lies in wait for desire, engulfs the other. I am that other. I am pure emotion lying in wait for the fate crouched inside this woman. The woman offers her desire, sows sentences in me whose syntax is unfamiliar and which I'm unable to follow and pronounce. Words there I cannot clearly distinguish – *breasts*, *gusts*, *ships*, *stext* – and, in between them, the woman's lips move like some life-giving water that cleanses away all clichés, promises that every imprint of the gaze will be sexual, will be repeated and fluid as vivid as the morning light absorbing one's most intimate thoughts. Her arms are open. She opens herself to the embraces that, in mother tongue, suspend reality. The woman has turned her head slightly and her throat astonishes. Her gaze contains traces of that water which, it is said, gushes when memory becomes verb and rekindles desire at the edge of the labia. The woman's gaze sweeps into the future.

CARLA: In Chapter Five, Descartes learns about Galileo's arrest. I have him say, 'I was afraid. And ashamed, for I had only just realized that it would to be too great a risk to publish *The World, or A Treatise on Light*. I did not wish to die prematurely in the fires of the Inquisition. I wasn't a hero. The truth could wait a few more years for an editor. Shame is a feeling I had never yet experienced, for until that day my actions and my thoughts had always been in accord. When we are made to face them, violence and injustice give a new configuration to the values that govern us.'

THE NARRATOR: How does the cardinal react?

CARLA: He doesn't. Hiljina is the one who intervenes by talking about guilt, honour and duty. For ten pages, she gives examples of courage and cowardice. I bring her progressively to talk about her mother, a peasant girl raped by the unknown soldiers of three different armies.

THE NARRATOR: Don't you think you're exaggerating?

CARLA: It was a common occurrence at the time. And rather more often than not. Why do you think settlers in New France sent their daughters to school with the Ursulines? Because it was simply the best way to keep them from getting raped before they were married.

THE NARRATOR: I didn't know you were interested in our history.

CARLA: Imagine what happens to me when I mix the words *Ohio, Detroit, Hochelaga* with some animal names and a few first names belonging to pallid people living along the highways of America and its great rivers. The stories that come from one era are all alike because of the tools and technologies. Morality being a technology of the spirit, it too spreads out everywhere at the same time. The boom of fascisms, the boom of dictatorships, the boom of fundamentalisms. For better and for worse, morality follows the stock exchange and fashion.

Joy, I imagine it takes joy to run up and down the long wooden staircase between the lower city and the upper city or to run full speed ahead in the alleys of Saint-Roch. I imagine it takes great joy to make the world come to life as though magically, in its everyday narrative, for people to be happily walking along Rue du Trésor, in the corridors of Parliament, in the cafeteria of Hôpital du Saint-Sacrement. Joy, it takes great joy to pretend you're not a people but just persons like everybody else; it takes great joy to open your arms out to the future, to new concepts and new complexes.

Since Mother's death, I often think about the men and women who are about to die. They aren't ill yet but I know they are going to be. It's a way of summarizing life, pitching it into the course of things with a joyful statistical curve. We add, we subtract. A generation leaves the city, another moves in, a third is already on its way. There's one image that keeps coming back to me since a gorgeous May afternoon when Mother was alive. We would always celebrate her birthday at an inn by the Richelieu River. We'd arrive for the one thirty seating. Sometimes we had to wait for the first seating to be finished, and I'd see full-bellied people, yawning, slowly preparing to leave, to yield their seats to happy, hungry newcomers wanting only to drink well and eat well – exact replicas of those now about to depart who, just a few hours earlier, had sat down at nicely set tables, consulted the menu with gusto, ordered dishes and wines that were still in the realm of the virtual and of desire. Now they were all sitting in front of stained tablecloths, of empty or half-empty plates, cutlery scattered about. In a few moments we would sit down, as happy as clams, in front of virgin tablecloths, pretty place settings, menus that would make us salivate. The maître d', the sommelier, the waitresses would repeat their courteous words, their mouth-watering explanations and their thoughtful gestures. We would feel like the first come, worthy of attention and respect. The first sip of wine would convince us of our immortality.

I imagine it takes joy about all things to rush into time and let it close in around us. Yes, one must doubtless allow time to swallow silence and the multiform narratives that surround us like a hedge of roses.

A xelle can see all these images flying by at the same rhythm as the traffic, slow but fluid: Lorraine choosing vegetables at the market, Lorraine driving her old Jeep and ranting against the pollution, the 'garages-motels' which, in her view, slow down the flow of cars. Lorraine preparing little canapés, cutting cubes of papaya for an evening to mobilize around the disappearance of two battered women. My mother at a reception at the Bellas Artes. My mother and father at the Cultural Conference in Havana. My mother in a little white cotton dress in front of a bust of José Martí, my grandmother in front of Jordi Bonet's mural at Place-des-Arts. My father holding me in his arms, sobbing, one referendum night.

People drive faster than in New Jersey. Axelle still can't decide whether she prefers the highways, discos and labs in Québec to those in the States. She doesn't know. For now, there are so many images in her head. The days are too short, the recent past as vast as the continent. An intriguing mix of vegetation where the hibiscus and armadillos of Coyoacán blend with the maple trees and squirrels of New England. A flashy past like the billboards in Mexico and those along the highways around Princeton where promises of eternity are exchanged with slogans like *Coca-Cola siempre, Coke always* and *Jesus loves you.*

What is an image of the past when it arrests you, holds up its hand and says in an authoritarian tone, *No entry*? Do you go around it gently, turn back or run for it headlong? Axelle glances in the rear-view mirror. Ahead, the sun slants, wan, harnessed to big galloping clouds. A two-and-a-half-hour drive, then the highly anticipated meeting with Simone, the discovery of Québec City. A northern city. A city of civil servants, she was often told at Princeton. A city she's never seen and has dreamed of since childhood. In the distance, a sky in heat. A life in the fast lane that doesn't allow Axelle to understand what made her decide to come back to Montréal, to add her foreign accent to a thousand others after all these years, young designer of sterilization and cloning for the better and for the worse of humanity. Tonight, let's rap *like hell*.

I take Carla's freedom for granted, and Simone Lambert's, and mine. It's still dark. A heavy rain is drenching the city. Standing behind the curtains I listen to the violence of the rain on the roofs, on the city. The water seeps into history, lifts up the earth, the grocery list a woman dropped when she darted into a fruit store. The sound of rain can be terrifying. I take for granted the freedom of water, the beauty of spring, the shade of the lilac trees yesterday, their fragrance. I take note, getting fired up about distant ruins. Rue Racine, rivulets form dark little lakes in potholes. During my first year in Québec City I couldn't fathom how the snow could stay so long, sometimes until May. I was chilled to the bone with grey. The rough surface of the stones irritated me. Now I'm everything-proof. The few emotions I feel, though intense, are powerless to nail me to dreams – I mean, to shut me down with a moist eye, tearful or trembling, in an altered state like dreaming or feverishness.

There are more and more tourists in town. Here and there, gangs of sad young things. Sad lads are like ruins covered with vegetation. Life goes on while they turn grey like the stones and their parents, khaki like tanks or simply invisible. I sometimes feel like talking with them, but sad lads don't talk much. They watch, they stand around for long periods of time, sit down for just as long, smoke and throw their butts into aluminum cans they squash with one hand if they feel like it. I also take for granted the freedom of sad lads.

Quite a number of us flirt with that dangerous and desirable thing, heat in the lower belly, a *force majeure* that can sweep away the static peaceful landscapes of the real in favour of the eternally renewed forces of wind and thirst.

The sad lads are indignant as they pet their dogs and wipe their pocket knives. I'm indignant about taking our freedom for granted. Since Mother's death, my violence has lessened. I strive to find better replies to pain. I carefully conceal them in the notices I'm writing for the museum. I like this camouflage, it throws shadows on the artworks and on my life.

She probably got back yesterday. Her office door is ajar. She's having a discussion with Fabrice and her secretary. I like knowing she's back. She asks me to come in for a moment. I ask how she is and answer all the questions put to me. Listening, scrutinizing, observing. Her hands, her mouth, the forehead, the sequence of gestures. I'd like to enter this woman's life and thoughts, take a quarter-century return trip in her company, circle her waist as we walk on Dufferin Terrace. Her office is strewn with little objects she's brought from Venice: masks, glass feathers, inkwells, leather notebooks. She offers me a glass feather. Turquoise. A feather, a turquoiserie. The librarian, who's also the director of special events, joins us. Simone offers her a mask. The mood is good. Fabrice unleashes his storytelling skills and off we go, across Piazza San Marco, to meet Casanova, who in turn immediately takes us to the Florian Bar where he becomes an even more charming, mocking good-looker smooth-talker. I look at Simone Lambert. I exist somewhere in her gaze but I don't know where, nor for how long. I stroke my turquoiserie. Casanova and the special-events director are laughing. Fabrice resumes his racy story. 'Changing centuries, changing sexes, changing names, changing everything in a lifetime without changing the verb.' Surely it's worth the gamble. I smile as I look at Simone Lambert. 'I love you' – Casanova, I wonder if he said it often, with varying intonations. Behind her a sky so blue as to stir the finest passions. Now Fabrice is describing how fate put into the master seducer's hands *The Mystical City of God* by Sister Maria of Jesus de Agreda, a book of bliss. Simone interrupts him by saying that, at the time, mystical fate took hold of whoever showed any kind of temperament. Having one's night of revelation was a must. Descartes experienced his triple dream the night of November 10, 1619, Marie de l'Incarnation her morning revelation on March 24, 1620, and Pascal his night of ecstasy and fire on November 23, 1654. Staging and setting are required in order to turn the pages of the calendar.

CARLA: Time must be allowed to flow between characters. There has to be trust, despite the risk of trends in things and in thoughts which, if too violent, can grab them by the throat, cut off their breathing or, if too light, isolate them in a gentleness unsuited to fiction. Over the years I've come to believe that the novel is nothing more than deconstructed time that falls back upon our shoulders like a first snowfall or soft dust. Hence this impression of finding oneself once again in a setting composed of the remains of one's own violence, of a pain both familiar and ancient which, in its moments of glory, allowed us to spit out the truth, to conceal the imperfection of the hours until their configuration changed. I've always thought my father saw his mother as if in a movie. Beautiful, gentle, anxious, a lock of hair falling over her forehead. A small woman who loved music and hoped to have many children. When he talked to me about her, he imitated her gaze, which he called sad and sinuous like the roads that wind round the lakes north of Stockholm yet keep the water out of sight. All of this he told me when, as a young adult, I still politely drank in his words. Someday you too – it happens to all of us – will talk to me about your mother, her face, about the time when, as a young girl, she surely wanted a future. Someday you'll talk to me about your childhood, about the first Montréal streets you had to cross alone to get to school. It's maddening to think how much our aspirations, fears and tastes are at the mercy of events depending on whether we're born ten years before or after the passing of a law, the construction of a metro, a cataclysm or a scientific discovery. I guess one must touch upon everything when telling a life: the toys, cars, dresses, hats, smells, crimes, the Saturday nights and Sunday afternoons. The music that blanketed all the things that made getting up worthwhile with the blue slowness of every morning. When Father talked about his mother, he looked straight ahead like at the movies. And I in turn saw him on the screen, walking with his back to me, hands in his pockets, in the rain. At the edge of the image was a street, and at the bottom of that street a large mirror, making it possible to avoid head-on collisions. Like fictional foliage, mysterious shapes made shadows on the mirror. I imagined, I translated into my own words what would have been untranslatable for others then.

Yesterday, while walking on the Plains of Abraham: I'm taking notes about the death throes of a black dog. The dog was limping when he appeared. He circled himself once, twice, before crashing against the foot of a maple tree where he softly groans. I'm taking notes while trying not to look at the dog's wound, even though I don't know which part of his body hurts most. It's a gorgeous day. The kind of May sky we spend winter months longing for. The wind is warm. It's Saturday morning. A couple of tourists and their young children walk over to the dog. Probably thinking it's mine, they ask me in English what happened. The woman becomes agitated. The youngest child wants to pet the animal. The mother stops him for reasons of hygiene. The man says, 'You should do something about it instead of taking notes.' He pronounces *notes* as though he were about to break into song. I tell him in French that we've noticed an increasing number of stray dogs on the Plains this year. The mother and children have started walking toward the ramparts. The dog must weigh about forty kilos. A handsome short-haired animal. His eyes are still open. Every so often his body quivers. Now I can see the wound. The blood is flowing bright scarlet on coal black. In the distance a man in uniform is coming toward me with long strides. I lose sight of the wound. I head for the statue of Jeanne d'Arc. Flowers all around it. Their names printed on little white cards. I transcribe their Latin names into my notes.

In Drummondville, Axelle has stopped for a coffee and a copy of *Le Devoir*. Since she's been back in Québec, she's finally developed the habit of reading every morning. At work, other researchers read only English-language newspapers. Reading *Le Devoir* reminds her of long conversations her father and mother used to have. Expressions come back to her: *avoir le nez long, le samedi de la matraque, être en beau joual*.

Axelle can see how they sprang into her head when Lorraine talked about it: great white horses, thick-coated shiny brown ones with threatening nostrils, eyes that frighten because they have a strange way of looking and you can't know what they see. The horse is a giant. One blow from the billy club, one kick and you can bleed to death lying on the pavement, head full of the demonstrators' cries, howls and swear words. You see legs, thick calves, Kodiak boots, sandals, running shoes. The cement is cold, rough, the asphalt smells oily, you hope nobody crushes your jaw. The fear of a hoof in the eye is paralyzing. You scream, you beg. Up there on his high horse, the policeman is out of reach. He thinks he's God. In his saddle, he is God for two hours.

The verb *piaffer*, to paw: this word always made her laugh out loud because of the two *f*s which gave the impression of wanting to splash. And the more her mother would laugh hearing her daughter's oh-so-coarse and sonorous laugh, the more Axelle would put it on, become a huge laugh machine. *To guffaw*. She could feel it swell in her chest, then rise up into her throat before heading back down, rolling rushing like a big rock all the way to the foot of her fear. *To jaw*. Lorraine also talked about demonstrations organized by women. Chained to each other so the police couldn't make individual arrests. *To paw*.

The twenty-four-page newspaper is lying on the table along with the tip. Axelle is on the road again, hoping the hotel has a pool and a weight room.

Sometimes funny ideas enter our heads and we end up believing we've been thinking about something important. I prefer people who think about their unlikely fears instead of their real solitude or their insane mothers. How is it we don't like to lie but we all end up doing it anyway – now to not hurt another, now to avoid, now to get to heaven.

Yesterday, Carla called me a passionate reader without knowing a thing about my reading habits. I think she meant I'm a passionate person and the word *reader* escaped her like a glass slips out of a hand. It's true that reading is part of my life, that it brings me pleasure, but at the same time it burns me. From the inside. As if, encountering my nostalgia, it ignites an unbearable elation in me.

I envy Carla for not being dependent on events. Her world is all interior. I need museums, streets, animated terraces. Books. I envy writers who still today are able to use the word *existence* while licking their lips, as if this were going to add meaning to life.

My encounters with Carla sometimes make me feel like writing. A chapter. Just one. No novel. No story. Just a chapter, a visual object with paragraphs, blank spaces, a vague whiteness of gesture as days go by.

CARLA: Water! Descartes wants water. He pleads and moans. As for me, I'm standing alone in a field of rape, yelling 'Water! Water!' like Christopher Columbus cried 'Land! Land!' when he saw Hispaniola. There's yellow all around me as far as the eye can see, under a sky of a blue so vivid it's been termed indescribable. I howl 'Water!' as if my final hour had come. This land is so flat I can see the curve of the earth. Descartes calms down. He gives the cardinal an authoritarian look and begs for a glass of wine. Faced with this contradiction, the cardinal doesn't react immediately. I take the opportunity to pull down my pants and pee while singing the first lines of an old sexist anthem, then I put everything on hold: gesture, song, crazy-lady act. And I act the cardinal, rolling my eyes. I let a gust of wind go by and then, in an unctuous tone, declare, '*Nunc est bibendum.*'

Simone Lambert is waiting, distracted, for me to speak. Behind her the river, a parking lot, grey and more grey, stone. The surface of her desk is bare. Nothing. Smooth as a screen. The world begins again at every moment, jostled by another more poignant one which immediately yields to another even more beautiful, more threatening, and so it goes until the present gives the impression of being a beautiful piece of cedar, its thousand facets streaming with light and promises.

Talking about my project isn't easy. I throw out a few names she recognizes with a frown. By turns astonished, curious and now intrigued by my words, she wants to know what motivates my great interest in vedutists.

– How does one describe the link between art and ruins? I ask. Ruins fascinate us. They force us into thinking about time, a sensuality of time as simple as *once upon a time by the seashore*, transparency, purity, nature in actual size. They are reminders, traces that, instead of making us ill at ease, bring us back to the future of our own ruins.

Of course I speak with enthusiasm while wondering what she sees in me, what I represent for her, or if I'm like a little rain so soft in the morning we confuse it with the grey weather or the still water in a basin. I'd like to ask her where culture begins and where the fear of death ends. I'm careful not to, claiming instead that both dreams and ruins are good at making us flirt with thoughts of a seductive elsewhere.

I stop talking. Simone Lambert promises to think about my proposal. I slip the word *dialogue* between us, then *décor*. We discuss theatre a moment. With a maternal mouth she recommends I consult a few treatises on architecture. She leans over to write (*description of Simone Lambert's hands, little veins, two age spots, a spiral-shaped gold ring on her left forefinger*): *The*

Book of Architecture, by Sebastiano Serlio, Milan, La Scala Theatre Museum. 'I can get you a special pass if you want to do research at the Canadian Centre for Architecture.' I nod, then other words circulate between us which bring us quite spontaneously to discussing perspective, lighting, ballets, shows and especially the first edition, dated 1486, of Vitruvius, the Roman architect who, rediscovered during the Renaissance, became all the rage by serving as a role model for many a young architect for finding pleasure in theory.

The images are vague. They appear slowly, one fragment at a time.

Axelle is driving fast. On either side of the road there are fields, grain silos. A few trees. She's reminded of her grandmother kneeling in the garden. Simone digging the soil with hands that look grafted on because her work gloves are so huge and pink. On her rounded back, the letters *MoMA* on the black of her T-shirt. The soles of her shoes are caked with earth so black one can imagine it being used to draw a backdrop for the August nights Axelle has declared the darkest of all because the stars seem to surge from some nameless opacity. At school two classmates teach her new words. A little Turkish girl has taught her *flowers, honey* and *Turkish delight*. As for the German girl, whose father is a biologist, she's already taught her, in addition to the words *Stein, Stern* and *Apfelsaft*, the words *shoulder blade, meniscus* and *cheek*. Axelle says Simone has a lot of cheek when planting flowers. Lorraine claims that all words help us to live, but we mustn't bend them this way and that like licorice ropes. Simone rubs her back and turns around, asking Axelle to scratch hard, there under the shoulder blade and a little bit over toward the spine. Axelle thinks her grandmother's shoulders are wide. She kisses her neck. The garden flowers are always big: no room for lilies-of-the-valley and bluebells. Here, we live among peonies, sunflowers and hydrangeas. Later in the day, Simone has promised to take Axelle to the Museum of Fine Arts to see the fat calves, toes, biceps and breasts depicted throughout time by great and mediocre artists. Some other day, promise, they'll spend time looking at the landscapes and portraits of nobles, queens and saints, military men and dark servant girls, most of whom time will have engulfed in anonymity and oblivion.

There were no other 'We'll go to the museum' times, only a parting kiss on the cheek one day in the main hall of an airport named after a fruit with people loudspeaking to announce a series of flights. Then there were cacti, hibiscuses, bougainvilleas in a little garden in Coyoacán. But no Simone.

Exiting history, exiting my own story as I please, seems infinitely desirable to me. To do so I juxtapose place names like Las Vegas, Salta or Trois-Rivières. I close my eyes, for I know I won't live there unless and until I've redrawn the landscape. Or else I simply head for the North and its mirror lakes that reflect bear jaws and great antlers. To exit my story, I imagine myself driving for hours through the pampas or the boreal forest. With every bump I glide into the scarlet round-ness of a sun on the brink of setting in the distance, as shacks made of tin and brown cardboard replace the green horizon and gradually turn into an industrial town whose residents are, for the moment, standing around in the heat, the dust or the cold, like people do in countries where dreams and their own histories never coincide. I sometimes tell myself it's not natural, all those men set in the dust, those women whose eyes we never see and whose visibility depends on the flamboyant colours of their skirts or the shape of the sleeping children on their backs or chests.

CARLA: Descartes is fourteen in 1610 when Caravaggio, aged forty, boards a felucca for Rome. Caravaggio dies in Porto Ercole a few days later after a prolonged agony on the beach of Versilia. I'm aware of your low tolerance for the word *agony*, but that's how it is. So Caravaggio's agony in the sand was probably a lot like Pasolini's on the beach in Ostia in 1975.

THE NARRATOR: I never said that the word *agony* horrifies me. I simply shared with you the fact that when Mother died, *agony* stopped being an empty word.

CARLA: (*signalling the waiter to bring her another Manhattan*) Lighting. Do you know the meaning of the word *lighting*? Imagine a pile of clean clothes on a washing machine in a laundromat. Sitting on a shaky chair, a woman in pink bermudas and a sleeveless beige shirt. Afternoon. It's hot. The woman is sweating. Outside there's a fine little drizzle. The woman lights a cigarette. Imagine the lighting on her face. A train station at dawn with people circulating, looking more or less computer-programmed. A woman in a jade wool cardigan stands looking up at the station clock. Her eyes are abnormally moist. Just above her hangs a huge neon sign which, should it fall as I'm talking to you, would kill her instantly. Imagine. A little car parked on the side of the highway. Once in a while an oncoming vehicle's headlights shine violently into it. A woman is sitting at the wheel. She's staring ahead intensely while masturbating. Imagine the muscles of her face when the headlights sweep over her gaze. Now move the ashtray and the glasses on the table, lean over the Arborite, wait until the image of your face is still and then describe your mother's face on her deathbed for me.

How cities infiltrate us so that we can no longer do without them will always remain a mystery to Simone Lambert. The colour of the changing river and its breeze, sometimes its violent wind, arouse in her a being on the edge who in every way resembles the image she has of the artist at her best yet whom she has always feared becoming.

Sun on her cheek, night sticking to her retinas, how many times has she, all abuzz with projects and memories, leaned her face against the bay window, pressed her being against the horizon, her gaze simply following the rose-lined paths leading to faraway sites where stone, marble and shells formed tiers of seats, nymphaeums, thermal baths, groupings so true to life they could have been a setting for her own. Why did the cities of Bosra, Petra and Palmyra come and spin around in her memory at the very moment Axelle was about to re-enter her life?

'I cannot, however, let this last vessel depart without ... It is true, even though you were the only thing in the world to which my heart was attached, he wished to separate us while you were still at the breast. And I struggled to keep you for almost twelve years.' Simone absent-mindedly leafs through the fourth volume of Marie de l'Incarnation's spiritual and historical writings. Marie's letters to her son have always deeply moved Simone. 'The circumstance that the Québec frigate is going to fish at the Île-Percée, where there are fishing vessels that return to France sooner than the vessels here are ready to depart, gives me the opportunity to write this little word ... These new habitants oblige us to study the Huron tongue to which I had not previously applied myself, having contented myself with knowing only that of the Algonquins and Montagnais who are always with us. You will perhaps laugh that at the age of fifty I am beginning to study a new tongue ... '

After she turned fifty, Simone too had started learning Spanish as if hoping, through this language, to reconnect with a Lorraine long since disappeared without a trace.

Tonight, everything in Simone is distraction, a chaos of images, volatile thoughts, a huge bone-crushing present which travels up and down the spine like her fear and discouragement when a competing museum tried to snatch artifacts she'd coveted for ages.

CARLA: These days you can't play at writing made-up stories. You have to aim directly at the goal and give the illusion of a continuous flow of thoughts that concern all of us, men and women, here and now. Out of the question to pretend, as in literature, where that's all there is, pretense in the midst of a great blur. Pretending until you're finally able to distinguish someone something that makes you feel like caressing or shutting up. It's a strange process, you know. When pages are flowing one from the other and there's no resistance, I'm surprised it doesn't draw me further into violence or into those zones of languor where the unspeakable remains skin-deep. When things just flow, I worry. And when words resist, I worry too that things are resisting so much, that words are putting up barricades and setting terrifying fires as if to keep me from rediscovering the perfection of July evenings and my mother's strong accent. So I lose patience, I get carried away. I let myself fall, bound and gagged, into the Wound (*see dictionary under* wound) as if I'd quite naturally learned to take my revenge on the dew and fine rains I readily associate with literature.

An alley of pylons drawn against the sky, satellite dishes above rectangular warehouses stocked with materials of all kinds, campgrounds filled with mobile homes where one imagines women and men playing cards and smoking, or a solitary individual leaning against an aluminum window frame, masturbating to chase away boredom more beige than a drop of sperm on kitchen flooring or a pair of underpants forgotten on a laundromat counter. And all along the way, here and there on the roadside like a repeated apparition, the same isolated tree in the middle of fields, assigned there to brave fate and the thunder and lightning of ancient gods who now refuse to watch over the new genetically modified corn. Axelle drives, fast, with little sparks in her eyes.

Traffic slows starting in Saint-Apollinaire. Something akin to panic overwhelms Axelle. Why did she agree to meet this woman who will probably want to question her about life in the days of her father and mother? A spirited sadness takes hold of her muscles and for a moment which seems like an eternity or a cliché, the past stretches out then retracts inside her, becomes rapid heartbeat. Suddenly on her right the Montmorency Falls appear like lightning, a repeated flash flood on which the eye cannot really rest because it's already captured by the gigantic shape of a bridge looming full speed ahead, juxtaposing itself upon the retina with the beauty of the landscape and vertigo. And suddenly, fear and uncertainty tie a knot so oddly voluptuous in Axelle's lower belly that she just allows herself to be rocked by the thought of seeing Simone again, the traveller, the brilliant director of a museum of civilization – in other words, a woman such as she's never known and who, because of family ties, must already probably love her, would probably have no choice but to love her.

CARLA: Sometimes I also played Queen Christina. But I always separated those scenes from those of Descartes's death. I, Christina, at full gallop through a forest of wheat and spikes which, the farther in I went, changed into crazy trees, those violently subjected to the wind. On other days I loved those scenes, so much so that I waited for dusk then ran out of my house and walked in the fields with the same fervour as the woman who every morning went through the numerous rooms of her castle in order to reach her library. Once there I would take a book out of my pocket and, pretending to read, I'd wait. Someone would knock at the door. I'd say: 'Enter, Mister Descartes (*in English in the text*). Please sit down and tell me about "that secret impulse which directs us to love one person rather than another."' On other days, I'd go hunting and systematically kill spiders, garter snakes and, with a bit of luck, every rat in my path. As Queen Christina I was admirably skilled and so cultured that it could have been said of me: 'She was so far removed from all the weaknesses of her sex and had so absolutely mastered all her passions.' In my novel, the queen lives in Rome and socializes with cardinals. Like Caravaggio, she dies in Rome.

Yesterday, I had an odd dream – they all are when they show us dying. A lion was holding his jaw open over my throat. He wasn't moving, just watching for the merest movement of my eyelashes. I was frozen in time and space, knowing full well that if I showed the slightest sign of life, that would be the end of me. Sentenced by the script, I woke up.

Let's get together again tomorrow afternoon at the Clarendon. I've something to tell you about Chapter Five.

Sauntering down Rue Couillard, I got the urge to enter a boutique whose window display was more attractive than the rest. Once inside I circled the shelves until, on a whim, I decided to buy a ring I glimpsed among several others. 'A poison ring,' the saleswoman said, 'from either Thailand or Indonesia or Asia,' while apologizing for her ignorance. The ring is made of silver. On each side are shapes that could be numbers or letters or a meaningless floral motif. The top, a domed cover, opens. Inside there is room for three heart pills or any other aspirin-type tablet that can treat those strange and mysterious maladies that darken the gaze of the living or take them away, for a brief moment's vertigo, to a better world. I bought the ring because of the word *poison*, which intrigues and fascinates me. I momentarily enjoyed toying with the idea that in just a few seconds you can go from one world to another, have death on your tail and down your throat, offer up your breath and your chest to fate. There's also the top, so highly polished it becomes a mini-mirror where I can see my anxious and slightly deformed face, like in some antique device for measuring anxiety that has remained suspended above the void.

I slid the ring onto my left ring finger. As I caressed the dose of imaginary possibilities contained in it, I thought fleetingly that something was going to happen to me. I like the ring. It makes me feel anxious. It tells me I haven't yet recovered from the images of Mother's agony. The ring reminds me that we are constantly walking through silences.

I don't dare tell Carla that I'm writing about our rendezvous. In fact, I've been transcribing our conversations for a month now. It all happened accidentally. I often record my comments about the works of art, the artists, the hanging or lighting of an exhibition. At home in the evening I translate my main points into written form. It was probably while rummaging through my bag one evening that I switched on the magic tape recorder, which captures the most silent vowels, coughs, low voices and even muted ones. Two hours of conversation including laughter, hesitations and, in the background, howling trumpets and demented saxophones. Carla tells her tales, gets ignited, laughs nervously. When I mention Simone Lambert she interrupts, saying, 'I hope you introduce us before I leave.' No matter what, Simone Lambert cuts a proud figure at the core of Carla's story. Yesterday, I played and replayed the fifth recording, taking the time and care to transcribe the most trifling exclamations that always punctuate conversations.

Ever since the first chance recording, I unfailingly slip the little device into one of my jacket pockets before meeting Carla Carlson. Two hours of conversation. Never more. Everything we say after those two hours disappears forever inside us, existing only in the inner being's infinite smallness. And lodges discretely in each one's memory.

Once home, I concentrate meticulously on the shifts in tone, the idling between words, the hesitations. I study the how of sentences, the birth of a topic, its strong points, its slow descent into insignificance or, on the contrary, its soaring to prominence in an overall pattern that creates the impression the soul is about to rise up against immensity. I don't feel I'm cheating or betraying. What I transcribe into my notebooks concerns only myself and language. The recordings sometimes make me

116

feel like there are three of us conversing, slowly circulating, moving toward the other, thinking, 'I'll get her, I'll get under her skin.' When Carla talks for more than twenty minutes without stopping I enter a rare time dimension which is neither hers nor mine but the time of literature, I believe. Time, art and reality inexplicably collect at the edges of our lips. Some evenings, Carla comes back to the fact that Samuel Beckett was once stabbed by a vagrant. I let her repeat herself, for just hearing Beckett's name moves me. On those evenings, I grab on to silence with a wristlock.

Fabrice just left for Istanbul. A few kilometres from there, preparations are being made to flood one of the most exquisite of Roman sites. 'They gobble up history like monkeys gobble and burp bananas.' Fabrice was angry-happy, radiant. As before every trip, he talked about ruins and gastronomy, about youths whose beauty is now classical, now sultanesque, or like a great cry in the mouth of a contemporary Saint Sebastian. We worked up until the very last minute before he leapt into a taxi for the airport. He left me at least a month's work while wishing me a nice summer. He plans to take advantage of the trip to holiday in Iran. As he was leaving he whispered in my ear that he plans to go to the theatre, outdoors and wherever the spectacle lures him. Three support staff came to see him off. They hugged and shook hands. Astri Reusch's sculpture felt whiter than usual and its watery murmur more harmonious.

It took me a long time to understand that human beings could find pleasure in one another. I long believed that only necessary things like work, sexuality and providing aid in times of emergency, in times of great disaster and uncontrollable fear, were at the root of all conversations. I always felt I was living in the margins of friendships, which must, they say, be cultivated and maintained with precautions infinitely more subtle than those required for love. Just like the word *agony* was unknown to me, friendship is, in its essence, I believe, foreign to me. This I discover while talking with Fabrice and Carla. Increasingly, Fabrice is something like a friend. He has that anxiety that often makes men worried and bony yet philosophical. Fabrice transforms his anxiety into a generous tenderness. He knows how to distinguish between true knowledge and the danger of half-baked learning rotting in the interstices of lucidity.

CARLA: At first I thought it would be simple. That it would be enough to make one character stand out and put the rest in her or his service. At first, Papa wandered through the streets. I decided on everything: whether he stumbled on a rock, slipped on the damp cobblestones, entered a bar, got drunk or not. I held his joy, his unhappiness, at the tip of my pen, just like, as a child, I'd held the destinies of Helen and Descartes in my voice, at the back of my throat, which I could fill at will with good or bad feelings. But I can't help it, I'm unable to talk about real life. For example, you see that woman over there, how when she aims her fork at her mouth she stretches her neck slightly, rounds her back, elbows tight against her breasts? That woman totally focused on the contents of her plate, which are now on the tip of her fork and now in her mouth, that short-haired plump woman with tanned chubby arms, is existing unawares. Those are the kinds of things I can't bring myself to write about.

THE NARRATOR: And yet there's nothing more fascinating than observing human beings. If, in addition, you're able to describe their most intimate gestures, you have the obligation, it seems to me, to respond to that call inside us to be curious about our own kind, be it only to act as a mirror or to foil a sense of hyper-vulnerability.

CARLA: You're probably right. There's an Italian writer whose books I always read simply because it's terribly hot in all his stories. In one of his novels the hero spends part of his time mopping his brow, eating omelettes and drinking lemonade. The heat destroys him every day. Life resumes at dawn and we get the sense that the man's soul is going to sink in the midst of culture or crash into a pile of garbage left on the curb. I like this author because his characters all suffer the sultriness without compromise.

THE NARRATOR: That seems rather trivial.

CARLA: To me it's stimulating. In struggling against the heat, this man is struggling against everything that makes life unbearable. It helps me understand. What's worse is that all this heat, all this anxiety, brings me pleasure. This is why I keep writing those dark novels against my will.

THE NARRATOR: So what are you complaining about?

CARLA: (*silence*)

Yesterday, after meeting with Carla: sooner or later everybody ends up saying 'I remember,' everybody without exception, anchored to their skeletons and to the pivotal moments of their life which, all in all, are not so numerous and never last more than a few hours, a few days at most. Pivotal moments proudly bequeathed to the next generation, which in turn will hand them down to the next one which will pin them to its resumé in lower- or upper-case letters every time there's a need to resist erasure. Carla often says, as though she were afraid of being forgotten: 'When the day comes that nobody on this planet is able to recognize your face in a photograph, you have just disappeared into the cosmic void forever.'

Over the last two weeks I've found conversations with Carla exhausting. There's nothing left between us but dialogue – a ball game useful for her novel but which leaves me isolated in centre field.

This frenzy for telling stories. The longer Carla stays, the more the novel progresses, the less space there is for me to insert myself into her world which, I'm sure, is going to devour her someday. Just ten years ago I would have noticed her rounded eyelids, like those of fifteenth-century Italian madonnas, the carmine lips; through her I would have awakened dozens of famous women: Joan of Arc and the Princess of Clèves, Catherine de' Medici, Marie Curie, Greta Garbo. Together we would have rambled on about learned women's lost sense of honour.

After a month of rendezvousing, Carla knows nothing of me. I am always presumed attentive and available. There's no doubt that I'm attracted by the disturbing landscape she carries inside her like a herizon. In this city of Québec, foreign to us both, we could have undertaken the countdown of certainties, set something up between us other than those existential play-things called childhood or flamboyant dreams.

She's watching me in the dawn's first light with an intensity that melts me. Her face a vivid world, I no longer know if I exist inside a photograph or if I once existed in the whiteness of the morning in front of this slow-gesturing woman who, never taking her eyes off me, is lying there in front of me, naked more naked than the night, more physical than a whole life spent caressing the beauty of the world. Sustaining her gaze is painful. I imagine, I breathe and imagine her once more. A few centimetres below the manubrium glints a little diamond that seems to stay on her chest by magic. The diamond, no doubt held there by a little ring inserted into the flesh, sparkles like a provocation, an object of light that lies in wait for desire, engulfs the other. I am that other. I am pure emotion lying in wait for the fate crouched inside this woman. The woman offers her desire, sows sentences in me whose syntax is unfamiliar and which I'm unable to follow and pronounce. Words there I cannot clearly distinguish – *breasts*, *gusts*, *ships*, *stext* – and, in between them, the woman's lips move like some life-giving water that cleanses away all clichés, promises that every imprint of the gaze will be sexual, will be repeated and fluid as vivid as the morning light absorbing one's most intimate thoughts. Her arms are open. She opens herself to the embraces that, in mother tongue, suspend reality. The woman has turned her head slightly and her throat astonishes. Her gaze contains traces of that water which, it is said, gushes when memory becomes verb and rekindles desire at the edge of the labia. The woman's gaze sweeps into the future.

Axelle is staying in a Sainte-Foy hotel. At the reception desk, a message from Simone welcomed her and set up a date for eight thirty in a restaurant in Rue Sainte-Ursule. Axelle asked not to be disturbed. She took a shower, then fell asleep with a large towel wrapped around her. She woke up famished, realized she wouldn't be able to hold off eating until her rendezvous, wolfed down two bags of nuts from the mini-bar. After walking around aimlessly for a while, she settled into bed to study a file on heredity. Two pages, she read only two pages before finding herself in Simone's arms, aged three. Her mother and father are having a discussion. She is leaning against the sink, he is pacing back and forth in the kitchen. Every time his heels hit the floor there's a funny sound. Simone recommends calm. Says the army can't just descend on people's homes like that without a search warrant or an arrest warrant. That happens only in dictatorships. Axelle remembers brushing her grandmother's cheek while trying to catch an earring that was shooting sparks across the dark kitchen décor. Her grandmother was crying. That evening she'd heard Lorraine and Simone talking in low tones as though they had only secrets to share. Axelle believed for a long time that she had the power to make her grandmother cry by brushing her cheek. (*Write three pages about the War Measures Act.*)

CARLA: It's never quite right to make a character disappear or die.

THE NARRATOR: Normally, somebody who's about to die has a serious look in their eyes and no longer makes grammatical errors.

CARLA: What do you know about it? These things are discovered through writing. You don't write, as far as I know – you're a writing virgin, *virgin in ink*, right?

THE NARRATOR: That doesn't stop me from having an opinion about the power of life and death that novelists claim to have over their characters.

CARLA: I admit I'm annoyed by people who, although they don't write, pretend to experience the joys and anxieties of writing. You either write or you don't – make a choice. Someone can't just be straddling the fence, in between two lives on the pretext that they're afraid of something that isn't them or that could become them if they did write.

THE NARRATOR: You have to be able to imagine, to encroach on somebody else's territory in order to promote certain verbs, for example the verb *to love*. If ever I do write, it will be only to tell a woman I love her and that she's the centre of the universe, where I try to grasp reality. This makes you laugh?

CARLA: No, but writers here can't seem to write more than five lines about stray dogs, so I wonder how they can write about love. In Europe, in the Caribbean and in Africa, you know as well as I do, a stray dog, what am I saying, stray dogs can take up half a manuscript. You know that in a European's eyes, someone who can't write more than five lines about dogs isn't a writer.

THE NARRATOR: I know. It's also necessary to know how to write about birds, faraway clouds, old furniture and the female body. Basically, writing about what intrigues us, makes us angry, enchants us and crushes us should be relatively easy. But if, as I believe, writing means slipping into the soul of a dog and coming out in people's consciousnesses in the middle of the night …

CARLA: The farm! A farm is an interesting place for that: pigs, weeds, you've no idea of the vocabulary you have to develop to describe cloud formations, the variability of lightning, its erratic designs through darkness. But it's true that I'd prefer to write about stray dogs, probably because I associate them with heat. The farm and the highway. Still, I like that. Strong winds of memory no matter where we speak from. Anywhere there are stray dogs and live chickens, there's dust and, in the end, all rogues lead to Rome. So, when Descartes is about to die, the cardinal ends up with bloodshot eyes and screams '*Alea jacta est*' as he rolls around on the floor like a damn fool. Because the wind is blowing toward the house, my mother can hear everything he says, everything I scream. She signals me to come in. I yell back that I want to stay here to fondle the night with my left hand. I want to do this like someone who writes, blending body parts with summer colours.

At eight o'clock, Axelle takes a taxi from the hotel. Just before the Porte Saint-Louis she decides to walk and asks the driver to drop her off in front of the Parc de la Francophonie, hoping to find there signs and symbols of an uplifting solidarity. The strange concrete structure leaves her pensive and the suspenseful effect of the word *francophonie* reminds her of when the Morelos family used to affectionately tease her about her funny *estraño* accent. Over the years the funny accent had become second nature and her mother tongue, though she speaks it more and more since living in Montréal, now has nothing in common with the firm choppy intonations typical of the exchanges between Lorraine and Alexandre when, using the words of everyday struggle and of life's pleasures, they blasted politicians' spinelessness. A bit farther on, a statue catches her attention. The sculpture recalls a postwar meeting between Churchill and Roosevelt. That the event had occurred here in this little provincial city of the North astonishes her. Then, the more she thinks of it, she tells herself that Québec City has no cause to envy cities like Oslo, Copenhagen, Helsinki or Stockholm, which she'd recently visited for a conference on women's fertility in times of war.

At eight thirty, Axelle enters the Saint-Amour. Simone Lambert hasn't arrived yet. Axelle is offered a seat under the big glass roof to enjoy a drink at the table reserved for them. She chooses to wait while walking along Rue Sainte-Ursule amid the peculiar old stone houses. At nine thirty, Simone Lambert still hasn't arrived. Axelle gets worried and impatient. This tardiness is about to turn into abandonment. Simultaneously hurt, angry and ready to forgive, eyes brimming with tears of sadness, she dashes into the street hoping a middle-aged woman will come up to her asking if she is indeed Axelle Carnavale, daughter of Lorraine Lambert.

In Rue Saint-Louis she turns left into the little Rue du Parloir, buys a diet bar and eats it while looking absent-mindedly at the grey stones of the Ursulines' convent. A day's-end kind of light runs over stone the colour of furry bunny wabbits watching at the edge of forests. The word *convent* starts spinning in her head, as familiar as a childhood object. Her mother, her grandmother, her aunts, each of them had at one time or another used the word to talk about that compulsory school-age rite of passage that gives young ladies access to the young men of Québec's small elite composed in those days of lawyers, notaries and doctors who would in turn become a pool for the class of political offspring of the years of 'The Great Darkness,' as her mother used to say and which her father used to translate as 'greatness darkened.' *Convent*: now the word was operating, cleaved to her lower belly, associated with walking long dark hallways, a music room and a panoply of forbidden places reminiscent of Violette Leduc's short novel.

On Rue des Jardins, a church that wears the name of a cathedral. Across the street, she walks along a pale-brick-brown building wafting a jazz tune she easily recognizes because of the Princeton nights where, as a part-time pianist, she accompanied a trio of jazzwomen for the sheer pleasure of sleepless nights. The handsome building intrigues her. On Rue Sainte-Anne, she realizes it's a hotel. An art deco–style lobby, verbless. As she enters, the cigarette smell rasps her throat. The smoky atmosphere reminds her of Lorraine's nervous chain-smoking gestures on meeting nights, when the house was full of men and women whose ideas ran red with change and revolution. At the back, a glass partition finely wrought with enigmatic flower motifs. Behind its transparency, shadows and the final notes of Duke Ellington's 'Sophisticated Lady.'

THE URNS

The museum is closed Monday evenings. Simone wanders through the great exhibition hall, where silence and solitude make an enticing couple. Since the very first days of the exhibition, she's made a habit of doing her rounds as a meditation in motion between the urns and the glassy reflections on the display cases. To the lilac of May and the river's changing blues she prefers the time bracket, the leap in time, represented by *Centuries So Far*. Even though she knows each piece in detail, its history, the site where it was discovered, its original use, Simone stands in front of them for a long while, thoughtful and fascinated, as though seeing them for the first time.

Once in a while the security guard's steps interrupt the purring of the temperature-control system, a purring sound that, in museums everywhere, paradoxically contributes to an impression of silence and intense mental activity, arousing in art lovers a sense of vitality.

Most of the urns are behind glass. Others, massive and scarred over their entire surface, appear under blond lighting produced by expert computation, making it possible to suspend time like an aesthetic particle over the debonair roundness of the giant urns.

Simone looks at the urns as if each one contained a small hard core which, while projecting her into the future, would also strangle her, a familiar nostalgia for when Alice, a young doctor, and Simone Lambert, archaeologist, roamed the world to gorge on sites, necropolises, volcanic sands. And on the sea. And on the sea. On that time when the short-term future always translated into a press conference to be organized, an article to write, an aperitif at sundown, lovemaking after nightfall when the darkness was so complete that it required her to listen constantly, closely, to lose nothing of Alice's pleasure

131

surrendered to the starless night, to the idea of infinity, while, not far from the campsite, jackals and hyraxes sharpened their appetites. Oh! How precious those times away on assignment, when Alice could escape the administrative dullness of the hospital and put a temporary distance between herself and intubated, palliative death, which she found cruel compared to the kind that once had reigned on the site, when swords, lances and daggers plunged endlessly into chests, viscera, eyes and any flesh crossing their path, leaving every grain of sand and blade of straw stained with blood avenged with blood shed.

On the sites, Simone did everything she could to ensure that, despite the harshness of the climate and the discomfort of the facilities, life was an expedition toward knowledge and the pure pleasure of existing in the light. In those circumstances Alice rarely talked to Simone about her work. Constantly occurring were accidents, little scratches, sprains, bites that didn't heal, raw wounds no one dared look at. Fevers. Some-times an anxiety attack would overcome a team member who would say they'd become enthralled with the devil or that the meaning of life had been injected into them like a slow poison. Alice saw to the fever and delirium. Simone would question the man or woman about the nature of the poison. When the person seemed able to listen, she'd say, 'Don't be afraid, it's just solitude at work. There's no poison in solitude. Quite the contrary, solitude is full of faces. The problem is, it affects the circulation of the blood in such an incoherent manner that thoughts are broken, torn apart. And this tear is what creates the confusion between solitude and the feeling of passion, sorry, I mean of poison.'

On those days, once the tools had been collected and put away, when the sun struck low across the marble and the ground seemed about to fly off like mysterious pollen over the graves and urns, Alice asked Simone if she'd used the Story of Cheatin' Luck to bring back to reason whoever had just escaped the throbbing vertigo of anxiety.

In the exhibition hall, Simone's thoughts sprang up pell-mell, came apart, dispersed quite naturally and came back now in a form that twinged the heart, lit straw fires of fury, caused sudden blindness. Faces went by, Lorraine's accompanied by those of Alexandre Carnavale, Trotsky, Marie Guyart, Champollion; then superimposed on Lorraine's face was Axelle's, her childish joy, her arms around Simone's neck so long ago. Sometimes the faces collided then took off again in all directions, leaving a torment, a pain, a knot here and there in the throat. The security guard's steps. What, in the end, is a life? What one has seen and told, what one avoids talking about or simply what one has invented and which has been lost over time, unbeknownst to us, very slowly just as one says a week has gone by already, the last day before your departure, three whole years of mad love, seven years of misery, a quarter of a century of war or a quarter of an hour spent waiting on a winter street corner for someone, something, that doesn't come, that won't come.

Passing by the urn called *royal*, Simone repeats to herself *urn, shoulder, belly, hip*. And suddenly water is streaming over Alice's firm body. Their life together reappears like an alternation of precious moments between the shortage of water on the sites of the past and the abundance of chlorinated water in the bathrooms of the hotels they stayed at on a regular basis: the cool water of the shower under which they multiplied their mouth to mouths, the boiling calming water of the hot tubs, the stimulating water jet they learned to aim accurately at their clitorises, which split time in two or, depending on circumstances, into a thousand fragments that splashed the eye and then gently went on to merge with the idea of happiness and the salt of tears. Urns of life and daily chores which, held at arm's length above women's heads, were illuminated by their energy or which, passing through their rough and wrinkled hands, poured tender milk into the mouth of a child or fresh water through an old mother's parched lips.

When at the sites, Simone often thought that in the light of day and the heat of the shimmering air she saw a far-off female form heading toward the east and toward her crimson colour until suddenly: a man catches up with the woman, yanks her by the arm which, forced to let go of the urn and its palmette, slumps, powerless and mute like an old sabre. The man drags the woman along. A cloud of dust replaces the human form. Simone would frown and her gaze would cut a path to the far-off woman so as to allow her to revel in her own luminosity.

Alice loved to watch Simone when she was so focused. It was this capacity of hers for observation and the faultless reliability of her judgment that made Simone so alluring. In the archaeologist's eye there was an indefinable something that brought to mind the far side of things, but as Alice couldn't look simultaneously at Simone and at the object of her gaze, she never quite succeeded in recognizing the objects of reality that crossed her field of vision. So when Simone plunged her black-irised eyes into Alice's, the latter could not absolutely guess which image was feeding, soothing, igniting her.

At Petra: Simone remembers shivering when, for the first time, she saw those tombs sculpted in pink sandstone now partly reverted to scar-faced raw material by the effects of sand and wind. When nature exhibited highly aesthetic scars, and especially when it reasserted itself over the artificial forms inflicted upon it, Simone always reacted with an emotion so vivid it often made her ill. Presently she recalled the Land Art that Lorraine was so crazy about and which had prompted their trips to Arizona and New Mexico. There they went looking for installations, sculptures, uncanny shapes, questioning the motivations, pride and merit of the men and women who practiced this outdoor art. A labour-intensive never-before-seen art full of artists' little fists rammed into the belly of a mountain. Cubes, rods and spirals drawn child-size in the vast, blinding desert. This unusual game went on and on. Just this morning, Simone had seen a picture of a New York artist standing like a little king in the middle of hundreds of naked bodies lying down in rows like merchandise, for the sole purpose of giving birth to an image wide open to being interpreted as the artificial cross-breeding of naked flesh and urban asphalt.

Later, at the sites in Karnak and in Bahrain, when touching the whiteness of time and bones with the tip of the soul was a necessity, Simone, already dealing with the ochre time of dusks and the mauve wind of dawns, had damned the god of her childhood and life who had taken Alice from her, her doctor, her learned woman of Sillery, who had never dared show anyone but Simone that amorous inclination which, when she surrendered to it, literally lifted her up from the ground and, in so doing, made her all the more desirable.

The security guard's steps have halted at the entrance of the exhibition hall. The man comes close enough to give the impression he wants a word with Simone. He greets her with a nod and then simply heads slowly back toward the silent *La Débâcle* to continue his rounds.

Hotels were the site of the better part of Simone and Alice's love life. There, each woman forgot her official life and their bodies sailed toward some elsewhere Simone sometimes regretted being unable to recount in a book. 'Oh, this is so good. Everybody should know what we do and want to do it too,' said Alice with such naïveté that it drew a smile from Simone. To preserve their anonymity, they had over the years constituted a bank of first names using the names of flowers and tried to match the number of stars given to a hotel with the number of syllables in the flower's name. Four stars: Petunia. Three stars: Violet. Two stars: Iris and Lily. For the surnames, they used only common ones like Tremblay, Vézina or Richard. For five-star hotels, they changed the rule and signed Iris Stein and Lily Globenski.

The ritual was always the same: hesitation, excitement, wild lust in the lobby, stolen kisses in the elevator, a guaranteed explosion of voices followed by a quiet river of tender words once the door had closed behind their coats, hats, gloves, dresses and jeans, their identities, with a multifaceted heat in the lower belly.

Standing in front of a black-faced hydra, Simone lingers a moment watching her face reflected in the display case. If it's true that when passing in front of a mirror we believe we can touch up our image by adjusting our hair, smoothing our eyebrows with a bit of saliva or licking our lips to redden them, it's just as true that looking at oneself intensely for longer than a minute is risky, as ten seconds are more than enough to know that those eyes are going to stop sparkling one day. So it's quite natural to think that an image of oneself is never identical to an image of oneself. And why stop? thinks Simone. Those who stop do it only to better refresh their life strategies, to rethink the management of their activities and assets or to detox from a heightened lust for life which has ended up marginalizing them. Nobody stops to forget. On the contrary, in order to forget one must charge ahead at top speed toward death like an athlete capable of setting any record. Thinking one's face can only be done outside the mirror frame.

Under the features of Simone's face is the child, the daughter. Lorraine's face. A birth. The pains have started. The belly is enormous. She can't see her feet. The belly hides everything. The pain tears the brain like major matters of fact that nobody talks about and, even if they did, there would be nothing other to do than give birth. Make soul of this body, beget future with every cell.

Behind a curtain a woman screams that she wants to die. The doctor says Simone is breathing well. Two men's heads hover over her. She can feel a nurse's reassuring gestures, then the gynecologist declares, 'Caesarean.' She says yes, anaesthesia, five, four, three. There was no two, no one, only a painful cough the next day and a Lorraine with jet-black hair and fists full of shadow and cosmic energy.

Putting a date on an event means in part acknowledging it. Simone didn't know anymore whether Lorraine was born at one in the morning, at 1:10 or at 1:20. From the depths of her artificial sleep, she couldn't know at what precise moment in history her daughter was born; had she known, she might have forgotten it like her own mother, who had never been able to tell the exact hour of the arrival into this world of her fifth daughter, in a room on Rue Drolet fragrant with the thousand odours of life and death. The only known fact was that Simone was born in 1929, shortly before her father left for Detroit and never came back.

The man could neither read nor write in French, but over the years he'd learned English, and when the war broke out, Simone, who must have been thirteen, remembered the mailman bringing long letters written by her dad about the year's new car models and what opinion they should have of them. Sometimes he included leaflets and calendars he put together with pictures he'd taken of 'big-shot' cars. In time he'd become 'calendar man' and year in year out the calendar, coveted by Simone's brothers and cousins, arrived via His Majesty's Royal Mail, the very same monarch in whose name they would soon go to war.

Over the years the Museum of the Automobile had made room for the work of Gustave Lambert, 'the French Canadian.' It included his first camera, a Kodak, and his last one, used mostly between 1945 and 1955. There were photos and newspaper articles about his collection. All the calendars from 1939 to 1954 were exhibited. To create a bit of ambience, they'd built a darkroom that had nothing dark about it but its name, the black walls papered with Coke and Camel posters as well as a postcard of Montréal. A life-size cardboard man stood holding a photograph in his right hand. The man wore black slacks, a white shirt and red suspenders. He was smiling. The picture of the cardboard man representing Gustave Lambert had been published several times in *La Presse* and *Le Petit Journal*. It was the only remaining image of him. Simone had a copy of it somewhere in a yellow calfskin suitcase, her memory box.

For years Simone had read up on the city of Detroit, its assembly plants, the famous Taylor Principle, which had inspired the model of the production line used in the factories: skills allocation, smallest combined expenditure of human effort, maximum utilization of tools and implements. And for a long time she had even used it herself on sites in order to manage her work teams.

Far is not the faraway, thought Simone. Here in my museum, far from my Montréal childhood and from what my life once was elsewhere, always elsewhere, I'm so close to what I really am in my relay race among civilizations and their gold and stone remains. To disappear in the mouth of stones that never embrace any shape but the wind, the cold, the incandescent heat of great lava slides down inclines and inclinations.

Despite their fragility, the urns have survived the centuries, protected by burial and lack of oxygen. Suddenly the title, *Centuries So Far*, that Simone had given the exhibition no longer seemed to apply to the past but indeed to the future, far-off centuries that would act as mirrors for other cultures belonging to our species. From the far reaches of these centuries, scholars would examine our ruins. Chernobyl and its children's park now silent with radiation, the Barents Sea and its underwater cities – far-off centuries where time and space would be implanted in the body as if a second level of time-space comprehension existed. Thoughts would go without saying, no longer needing the lengthy processing via speech that so often complicates relationships. The notion of tomorrow, the sense of today. Desire, a lapse in time, a *lapsus linguae* folded underarm like a personal journal. Would the subjective time that resurfaces whenever a new technology outperforms an older one resemble a woman's belly, against which one can set one's own silence and certain notions about becoming among the stars? Whoever took the time today to see the ruins of tomorrow coming would guarantee their own financial future. The ruins of the ephemeral would grow in number.

Henceforth, multidirectional time could change direction at any moment, turn on itself, bolt back to the past, return to same, morph into a hacker and neatly ruin our linear lives.

Eight-oh-four and ten seconds in the evening. The news came via Simone's cellphone like an axe blow to the ear. The news fell into her phone like a two-year-old from the fifth floor the news fell into her phone like a knife slash into the gums the news made a blackfly buzz in the phone the news spread through Simone's body spilled tons of toxins into her brain left a trickle of saliva at the corner of her mouth unravelled the quiet thread of life the news sent shivers down Simone's spine nailed her to the front of Niche Number 7 of *Centuries So Far*. The security guard reappeared in the entrance, hesitating because of Simone's haggard look. Fabrice Lacoste had just been found lifeless in a pine grove on one of the Princes Islands (*Buyükada in Turkish, Prinkipos in Greek*) not far from the Bosporus. His body had been discovered at dawn by a Turkish-delight vendor who happened to pass by. The corpse showed traces of violence, of origin currently unknown. The remains couldn't be sent home before the end of the inquest. The Canadian Embassy had just phoned Fabrice's sister. 'Can I do something to help?' asked Simone. 'Not right now, thank you. I'd appreciate it if you'd pass the news on to the people who loved him. I'm leaving for Istanbul tomorrow with my husband. You can reach me at the Kybele Hotel. In Québec City, my sister Louise will provide you with more information as soon as she can.'

Half an hour later, movement returns. Simone goes back to her office. She makes a few calls. It is still daylight on Rue Dalhousie when she leaves the museum. She takes Rue Saint-Pierre toward Rue Saint-Paul. In front of the Dominion Hotel, two senior civil servants from the culture ministry are talking and gesturing. A throng of tourists has gathered around a stone sculpture by Arnoldin, Hébert and Purdy. The fountain water flows gently under the impassive female figure bearing foodstuffs. Daylight is dimming. The smell of erasure, thinks

Simone, who after turning back now takes Rue du Saut-au-Matelot to Côte de la Montagne. Up there, the cannons parked in rows look like great black wolves howling at the moon. She walks by the obsessive ghost of the Château Frontenac, heads for Dufferin Terrace, sits briefly under a belvedere that looks out over the river. Around her people are drinking soft drinks or licking ice cream cones and studding their speech with anglicisms. She notices a stain on her suit. She passes her hand automatically over her knees several times. Then, with an anxious look, she slowly heads toward the great wooden staircase leading to Cap Diamant. Then come the Plains of Abraham, where she walks round and round for an hour, feeling like an easy target. In the evening's tenderness, she chooses to hang her head and concentrate on the pebbles lodging in her sandals and the dew-laden grass tickling her toes. Then, in the middle of a sentence obsessing her, she raises her head, retraces her steps. On Dufferin Terrace, a street clown is crooning to docile dogs heartily applauded by a crowd standing in a semicircle and blocking the way of people who, like Simone, don't quite know where to go and whose hearts are as heavy as a dictionary full of useless words. Ten minutes later, just as Simone is about to hail a taxi, a woman brushes against her arm. Looking up at her, Simone notices that the lights of Lévis have started to glimmer like little monkeys with sparkly-bright eyes. The softness of the wind. The sudden fragrance of lilac season snaps her thoughts back to the past. May turns your head. Life. Simone doesn't complete her movement, the taxi drives by. With a determined step she heads for the Hotel Clarendon like, so long ago, Lily Globenski breathlessly loved to do with Iris Stein.

THE HOTEL CLARENDON

The bar (or a festive occasion) as setting always fuels expectations. The alcohol served can at any moment loosen tongues and incite them to the delirium of truth. All conflicts are possible, they just need to be framed, revived, sometimes left to burn onstage like a pile of debris. How to fan a conflict so as to render it exemplary is a matter that doesn't concern us here.

We are in front of four female characters. There is a family tie between the youngest one (Axelle) and the oldest one (Simone), a work relationship exists between the latter and the narrator, and a circumstantial relation based on affinities has developed between Carla and the narrator.

The fact that there is no conflict-generating factor (competition, antagonism, discord) between these women makes it particularly difficult to provide the script with moments of extreme tension, even of the verbal violence on which theatre is generally predicated. Indeed, there are no couples here, no visceral connections nor passion-driven ties. No jealousy, hatred, love. No intimacy, no daily life between the characters. In addition, one may wonder when, at which degree of intimacy, major conflicts, meaning those whose scope is symbolic, are born.

Talking is an activity that helps overcome solitude. In the theatre, talking goes without saying and is never quite useless. Certainly, there is a kind of theatre in which, under the guise of trivial sentences, there is allowed to smoulder a powerful fire that can blow into a terrifying explosion at any moment.

The lighting: as in museums, lighting plays a major role here. In the bar it can be a translucent white but also that yellow reminiscent of the tiny holes of city lights glimmering in a room, a living room or a kitchen. It's the magic of lighting that brings the landscape of reality into existence. Here, reality is absolutely theatrical. That is the wager made. On the faces, the lighting can be either blunt or caressing.

The sound: a digital soundtrack composed of murmurs, whispers, breathing and heartbeats. A few isolated words, repeated like serial patterns. Jazz tunes hang in the air, now and then a melody.

The last notes of 'Sophisticated Lady' are heard. The art deco–style bar of the Hotel Clarendon, renowned for its jazz evenings. Depending on the night, performers are jolly old musicians, hot young composers and, occasionally, female singers whose voices waft like cicadas and the blues. In the middle of the room, a piano surrounded by a semicircular counter and four stools. Tables, chairs. Very little smoke. One of the tables is occupied by the narrator and Carla Carlson, deep in conversation. For the moment it is impossible to hear their words. People arrive and sit at the other tables.

Axelle Carnavale enters the bar. All the tables are occupied. She hesitates a moment, then heads for the narrator and Carla's table where, after a brief exchange, she sits down discreetly, as far away as possible in order not to disturb. The narrator and Carla continue their conversation. Axelle cannot hear what is being said, for the words get lost here and there in the fluid brouhaha of the music and of the fluted resonance of clattering glasses and silverware.

SCENE ONE

CARLA: You can never know what's going to happen to a character. What fiction will make him say or not. All we know is that the character's life is always in peril. That danger lurks and that it organizes his destiny, designs his gestures, stokes his desire. The character often talks loudly because he absolutely must attract attention to himself, stand out from those who are going their own sweet way, life size, simple size.

NARRATOR: And if the character is a woman – does it make any difference if the character is a woman?

CARLA: Nothing obliges us to think that a feminine character is necessarily a woman.

NARRATOR: You've got to be kidding!

CARLA: Absolutely not. It's quite possible to live in the feminine and hate women. To love one's mother like a god and find other women unbearable. Pardon the expression, but a lot of philosophers spend all their time sucking on this subject as if it had a special flavour. It's both simple and complicated. Take me, for example: I work with the idea that Father my papa the old man the lassoed one is a feminine character. Any character who lives at the heart of his childhood can be said to be feminine. As soon as he leaves there he starts getting on in age, in dullness as well as in the dust of adulthood and dailiness. You see, this is the contradiction that works on us like a bad spell. Everybody is moved by the feminine's infinite tenderness, but nobody is interested in women.

146

(Simone enters, sits at the bar. Nods to the people around her. The audience can hear the conversation between Carla and the narrator, but not Simone.)

CARLA: The obligation to make a character speak transforms his nature. We don't know anything about a character until we've seen him exist in his body, until we've heard him talk, made him talk, seen him smile, cry, scream, breathe. Mince and swallow his words.

NARRATOR: All of that can be described, no?

CARLA: I know, but it's not the same. A character never pretends to be alive: he is alive. He can die in front of you at any time.

NARRATOR: I've always imagined theatre characters as tender beings capable of adapting to any game of smoke and mirrors, and even to false embraces, while reality coils round them like exuberant ivy or an inescapable story.

CARLA: Theatre characters are often violent because they're under constant threat. Their violence is proportionate to their fragility. The more they attempt to escape fiction, the harder and more merciless they become. You still refuse to read my manuscript?

NARRATOR: Yes, Carla. For the moment, I don't want to read anything.

SCENE TWO

(Simone gets up to make a phone call. Spotting the narrator, she absent-mindedly nods to her. When she returns, the narrator approaches Simone. We understand that she is inviting her to sit at their table. Simone accepts.)

NARRATOR: This is Carla Carlson from Saskatoon. Novelist. She never talks about us in her novels but always comes here to finish her manuscripts by the river, at close quarters with our history. Carla, this is Simone Lambert, director of the Museum of Civilization.

SIMONE: We welcome you within the walls of our collective memory and of our tourist-friendly citadel. *(Simone looks briefly at the narrator. The ambient noise decreases, gradually ceasing.)* I received a phone call about two hours ago. About Fabrice. It was to tell me that he ... it was to tell me that his body had been found in a pine grove on Princes Island near Istanbul. He'd been dead for fifteen hours. I spoke with his sister. For now there's nothing to do but wait.

black hole [falling into time, into the pure fiction of every sudden and unexpected disappearance. A wrenching apart. Everywhere in the world, people scrub objects. Everywhere in life, women wash bodies, clothes and objects. Everywhere, bodies disappear after having been examined, washed, embalmed, their strange fixedness examined one last time by an other who, throat knotted and eyes alight with thoughts of revenge or infinite sadness, gets lost in a darkness that none of his habits had prepared him for. The bad news rushes to the brain / cuts

off the electricity, then, in one jump, steers toward the dark side
of entrails, of saliva and of tears where there are no words to
translate]
black hole impossible to cross

NARRATOR: Wait for what? For him to come back from the
dead?

CARLA: Who is Fabrice?

SIMONE: I'm sorry. There's no good way to announce someone's death. Fabrice is dead. (*silence*) I'm exhausted. I had a date
with my granddaughter. I've not seen her for such a long time. I
wouldn't recognize her. (*She says this as she looks at Axelle. From
this moment on, the young woman seems to find some interest in the
conversation. Little by little, it becomes obvious she has recognized
Simone Lambert.*)

CARLA: You don't have any pictures of her?

SIMONE: We were to meet in a restaurant not far from here.
The news of Fabrice's death threw me into an altered fate, oh
sorry, I mean altered state. I came in here out of habit. Deaths
are multiplying, we're so unaware.

NARRATOR: How did he die?

CARLA: Who is Fab–?

NARRATOR: (*annoyed*) The museum's chief curator.

SIMONE: We don't know. I don't know. His sister didn't know
anything. I tried to reach the embassy. The offices were all
closed. Are you familiar with nights along the Bosporus? At
this time of year they're soft enough to hurt you, to make the

most beautiful images of your life resurface. The night fills with mysterious sounds and you spend it with strangers as though it were the only thing to do. You're afraid of nothing, you're happy, while in the perfumed night your eyes seek a name for each star, a word with which to catch the wind of madness that stirs in you as you try to understand how it is that, with your body pressed against memory, you still can't manage to feel anything but pure present. (*turning to Carla*) You're from Saskatchewan?

CARLA: By birth, if you will. But I gave myself a French style so long ago that I'm the only one who knows where I come from.

SIMONE: What do you mean by *French style*?

CARLA: A way of imagining that the world is yours and awaits only a word from you to exist.

SIMONE: I can see that you've travelled a lot or read a lot. Travelling and reading, it's true, have that ability to change us to the extent that we sometimes end up taking ourselves for someone else. Nietzsche, for example, liked to pass himself off as a Polish count.

CARLA: It's because of my mother. Without her, I'd never have taken myself for someone else. She talked to me constantly about René Descartes, who'd come to Stockholm especially, so she said, to die at the court of Queen Christina. One day I saw a film starring Catherine Deneuve. I was eight years old. From that moment on I became interested in France. I started stealing my mother's lipstick and playing the parts of flaming drag queens. Later on I started calling, with loud swordplay, for the head of a cardinal whose portrait I'd seen in a little French-Canadian girl's school book. My sword gradually turned into a sabre and I saw myself navigating the Atlantic with a parrot on each shoulder.

NARRATOR: I can't quite believe that Fabrice is dead. Wham! Bang! Gone. Just like that. Slam! Just like that, a twist of fate. Slam! Here is a man, here is a corpse. Death swallows hard.

SIMONE: Calm down. Were you very close?

NARRATOR: I drove down to Montréal with him sometimes. We discussed theatre, painting, travelling. He didn't talk about himself much. I mean, about his private life. He was a man who cultivated his gestures and his voice. His wounds, too. There was nothing natural about him.

SIMONE: (*as if she'd not listened to the answer*) It's the third time.

NARRATOR: The third time what?

SIMONE: Sudden deaths destroy. I mean, the life of the men and women who remain behind. Sudden death is like a huge pin that impales what's most precious in us, and that's not the heart. When death, a sudden one, looms, in one fell swoop it lacerates everything you have of skin, of pitiful skin, to protect you against time and the wicked eyes of fate that want only to swallow you up in one gulp. The day I learned of my daughter's disappearance, I fainted. Six hours later I was on a plane heading for Mexico. It was July. Torrential rains had started to erase everything. Car tracks, truck tracks, dogs. Streams of mud everywhere. The heat made me feverish. I was returning to a country I knew well for having loved it, kneeling in the stony ground under a blazing sun, searching the earth, using a pick-axe and my hands in sandy ochre-coloured mud hoping to meet the sharp onyx stare of a jaguar or the shiny scales of a serpent-god. (*silence*) I'm sorry.

CARLA: Suffering that keeps us halfway between misfortune and fiction is a foul thing. Sometimes it seems tailor-made to bleed us of all our blood.

SIMONE: Are you superstitious?

CARLA: No, I'm a novelist. I cultivate a bare minimum of humour so I'm not left cowering in pain.

SCENE THREE

(The last bars of 'I've Got a Date with a Dream' are heard. Applause. Musicians' break. Axelle orders an orange juice in French. The waitress says, in English, 'One orange juice.' Axelle repeats, 'Oui, un jus d'orange, s'il vous plaît.' She pronounces each syllable carefully, as if she were making a political statement.)

NARRATOR: I thought you were single.

SIMONE: I am by nature.

NARRATOR: It's strange, imagining you as a mother, as a grand-mother especially.

SIMONE: There's no point making a big deal of it. I should go back to make a call. I don't know anything about her. This whole story is absurd. I feel like I'm living a story that doesn't belong to me.

AXELLE: *(interested in the conversation)* Excuse me, would you have a pencil I can borrow?

CARLA: Are you from here? Are you here as a tourist? Like me?

AXELLE: I'm attending a conference.

SIMONE: You're very young.

AXELLE: Is that a problem?

153

SIMONE: It was a compliment.

(Feeling uncomfortable, Axelle goes back to her seat at the end of the table.)

CARLA: My whole life I've dreamed of living as a stranger. I feel good only when I'm somewhere else. It's like at the theatre – the plays I like always happen between strangers, never in families.

NARRATOR: 'Families, I hate you'; *Electra; Hamlet; Marcel Pursued by the Hounds; Cross Purpose; Suddenly, Last Summer*. If it's drama and tragedy you want, then stick with family, where hatred and the proprietary instinct are ever so fertile.

SIMONE: You're probably neglecting some very fertile ground there, Carla.

CARLA: The curse on my writing is that I grew up in a happy family. So I'm reduced to inventing my father and my mother as these peculiar objects who could be the cause of fireworks, verbal explosions, mysterious whisperings.

NARRATOR: You're exaggerating. (*in a tone of sympathy*) Write what you must and don't bother us with your happy family. Anyway, happy family or not, we always end up in mourning for our mothers.

SIMONE: Do you still have your parents? I mean, are they still alive?

NARRATOR: My mother died two years ago. Since then I left Montréal to come and work here, in your museum. You know, Simone, it's a pleasure working with you, for you, if you prefer. (*Axelle raises her head when she hears Simone's name.*) That exhibition project I spoke to you about a while ago, it matters to me.

A lot. I'd need special permission to consult some documents in the library at the Canadian Centre for Architecture.

SIMONE: Let's talk about work some other day, if you don't mind. I'm weary. Let's enjoy the music and the night. Have you known Carla for a long time? (*without giving her time to reply*) I find her quite pleasant. I dreamed of being a novelist for a long time. Now that I've reached a respectable age to write my memoirs, the desire for novelizing has gone. In any case, novelizing isn't really very trendy anymore. Today, one must document. Everything. People seem to want to consume things raw. Events, emotions, actions. Nothing reheated. Everything's got to be raw. You have to 'get it' unprepared, in real time, where, as we know, nothing particularly interesting happens except that in principle we're there without really being there.

CARLA: Once something is written – an action, for example, 'Simone gets herself a glass of water while absent-mindedly looking out the window,' or a sensation, 'the house is fragrant with a good coffee smell' – once written down and especially once in print, the sentence will never again exist in real time. It forever goes over to the side of fiction – that is, where we are not, which by the same token forces us to imagine in order to understand. Because of this phenomenon, which constitutes the very miracle of literature, quite a few contemporary novelists don't question the interest that their every move, rant and most meaningless sigh can elicit, once documented in writing. You're right, Simone, today we document everything as if it were necessary to collect our each and every thought and action to avoid being swallowed by the eternal present that flattens everything in its path.

NARRATOR: *Ruins: Time's Remains, Desire's Reign*. That's what I'd like to call the exhibition. Do you know the book entitled *The Lure of the Sea*? The text harbours a major, a subterranean, nostalgia that highlights fatal words like *suicide, monster, catastrophe. Gloom.* Don't laugh. *Gloom* is a contemporary word just like *erratic blocks* or *natural abysses* are expressions that accompany our everyday lives.

CARLA: Wouldn't it be simpler to say *daily lives*?

NARRATOR: Our everyday lives are not daily. If they were, we wouldn't fear the void. There's something restful about the word *daily* while *everyday* is like a warning, as if misfortune could befall us at any moment, at any hour, and eliminate us with a whack of its paw and of fate.

SIMONE: (*in a detached and benevolent tone*) What do you like about that book?

NARRATOR: Seascapes and their fantasy-inspiring coasts. The book drowns the sea in its own spectacle with its dykes, shores, storms, shipwrecks and immensity. It places the meeting of body and sea above all else – it takes the soul by surprise. Time is a landscape for travellers open to the idea of wounds ... (*The narrator sinks into her thoughts then concludes as though she had finally found the right word.*) It's a book open to the idea of vestiges.

(*The musicians set up.*)

CARLA: What an odd expression, (*pensive*) 'a book open to the idea of vertigos.'

SIMONE: Of *vestiges*.

(*The music starts. Carla and the narrator signal Axelle to come closer.*)

NARRATOR: Do you think we're truly ourselves when we're dreaming?

CARLA: Who else would we be? We're always ourselves, regardless of circumstances, regardless of whether we're busy lying, cheating, assassinating, telling the truth or playing Pirandello. There's no real flight, but one can play at something, to be sure. I like the idea of makeup, of deceitful mimicry.

SIMONE: Of masks and masquerades. 'Starting in the sixth century, Thespis smears his actor with wine and white lead or hides him under a white sheet. In the fifth century, Phrynichos imposes the mask for feminine roles, then Aeschylus perfects it [...] One of the ancient masks is called the Gorgoneion. Hesiod writes that the Gorgons, the most famous of whom is Medusa, are three monstrous sisters, daughters of the Old Man of the Sea. Their abysmal faces (round face swollen with anger, serpent-hair, flat nose, huge mouth) stupefy whomever looks upon them. Perseus, when he wants to deliver Andromeda from her rock, beheads Medusa, taking care to not set eyes upon her by using a mirror, carries her head away in a bag and uses it as a weapon to petrify Andromeda's monster guardian.'

AXELLE: I'm sure we all have a virtual 'me' inside that offers the hope of not always being oneself.

NARRATOR: Ask for your virtual 'me'! Clone of my mother, tell me who's the fairest, will the real me be this one here or that one over there?

AXELLE: Don't make fun.

SIMONE: 'The mask's function is to cancel the effects of time and time itself.'

CARLA: Everything changes so fast. That _____ distresses me. On some days we tell ourselves nothing has really changed, that we're still the same. Wrong! We're so pressed for time. Pressed like lemons, plugged into ever-newer novelty. Being pressed without being in a state of emergency changes our nature. We are the new serfs. Well-connected. (*turning to Axelle*) What's your name? Shall we use our first names?

AXELLE: Axelle.

(*Simone looks at her intensely. Axelle looks away.*)

SIMONE: That's an unusual name.

CARLA: There was a Swedish figure skater with that name.

AXELLE: My mother used to tell me about him when I was a child.

SIMONE: (*whose voice has just changed*) A few years ago, Fabrice Lacoste wanted to curate an exhibition of Venetian masks. I was against it. With all my being I was against it. I felt there was something futile about such a display of masks, which seemed to me to be nothing more than traps for seduction, lies and perversion. Back then I just didn't have the playful spirit I do now; and yet, as the months went by, Fabrice managed to convince me. We're unaware of the extent to which pain, or, rather, the will to avoid suffering, dictates our choices, our opinions, commands our decisions. I was travelling a lot in those days. A woman friend often accompanied me. That year we were supposed to go to Venice. It was February, a time of the year when part of the city is flooded, damp and cold. Regardless of the work awaiting me there, we'd decided that this trip would be unforgettable and wagered that we'd be able to transform the rain and fog into a spectacle of the pure pleasure of life. Departure was two days away. Suitcases were packed and standing in a corner of the living room like two handsome purebred dogs. In a few minutes, night and its old inky silence would own the landscape. Standing in front of the window, I was looking at the river and Lévis while talking about the Grand Canal and Cannaregio. I could feel Alice's movements behind me, coming and going around the table where we'd soon sit down to a favourite meal, with smoked salmon and *prosecco*. Sometimes the reflection of her joyful body appeared in the bay window, then immediately disappeared to make room for the lights sparkling on the opposite shore. I remember a noise, light wobbling. I turned toward Alice. She was falling, falling in slow motion her heart beating her cheek striking the floor hard in slow motion Alice's soul flooding the whole room, embracing me. Alice died two days later, surrounded by her husband and two children. As far as the family and the hospital were concerned, I didn't exist. Besides, I did nothing to exist in their eyes. I never sought to make noise about our relationship. That year, for I don't know what reason, the streets of Québec were bare of snow. I remember walking part of the night through the city streets, which had become quite foreign to me. Under my boots I could feel the grains of sand and of salt break up with a continuous and nervous squeaky crunch. The fact that there was no snow as usual stirred a feeling of inexplicable fright in me. I walked part of the night then came here to sleep in this very hotel where I was known as Iris Stein. Twenty years later, when Fabrice first talked to me about his project of an exhibition of masks, all I could do was howl my disapproval.

NARRATOR: (*to herself*) Fascinating, this sense of well-being and of worry that sets in when someone casually tells a story that creates the impression of having wind in her sails and solitude tightly packed at the bottom of a powder keg.

CARLA: Yesterday, I listened to the bells of a church in Saint-Roch for a few minutes. I was certain I was thinking about nothing when I saw myself again in Saskatoon, on a May day, sitting on a bench facing the river, which was rippling with a mixture of exquisite words whose meaning was emphasized now by the wind, now by light and the continual rustling of insects still plentiful at that time of year. The day was perfect, the sky absolutely blue. I was thinking about my mother going back to Sweden after my father's death. Every time a person dies, another one goes somewhere else. It's as though death constantly displaces populations. I was thinking about my mother, and the idea came to me to create characters whose speech, although contemporary, would nonetheless have made them anachronistic. Perhaps for me it was an entirely natural way of foiling sadness and reframing it in a more tolerable land-scape. The characters had paraded in front of me, then, as in my childhood, I'd made them disappear by taking their place. On that perfect day's morning, I'd seemed to myself like one of those undefined and troubling masses in Francis Bacon paintings. I'd become as yellow as death.

NARRATOR: No civilization associates yellow with death.

SIMONE: Not so fast! 'Yellow is the colour of eternal life like gold is the metal of eternal life. It is also through these golds, these yellows, that Catholic priests lead the dead to eternal life. In Egyptian funerary chambers, the colour yellow is the one most often associated with blue, to ensure the soul's survival, for the gold it represents is the Sun's flesh and that of the gods.'

AXELLE: I'm sorry but I can't follow. I don't understand anything you're saying.

CARLA: Nor do I. That's why I like this idea of cheating on reality so much.

(Simone turns to Axelle and whispers something inaudible to the audience.)

(Simone and Axelle are seated at the table, while the narrator and Carla are now standing by the piano, listening to the music. The dialogues will alternate between table and piano.)

SIMONE: Do you like jazz?

AXELLE: I'm here by default. I had an appointment that fell through.

SIMONE: Me too. I was supposed to meet someone your age.

AXELLE: It's my first visit to Québec City. I'm a native of Montréal but I didn't grow up in Québec. It's like a foreign country. Sometimes images from the past come back, but I can't tell if it's something I read or lived. My work is demanding. I've little time to think about my origins. In any case, in twenty years' time, who is going to be able to talk about their cultural origins with any certainty?

SIMONE: The person I was supposed to meet … you know, I rarely have the opportunity to talk with someone your age.

AXELLE: I spend a lot of time with people older than I am. Most of them could be my parents, in fact.

SIMONE: Does it bother you?

AXELLE: I don't really pay much attention. Except when they look down at me. I usually meet people for work. I just try to be efficient and expect the same from others. I don't like to be taken for just a young woman. It keeps me from reflecting, from thinking.

SIMONE: Thinking straight, as the saying goes.

AXELLE: Thinking, period. For example, I don't know you, but you may already be wondering if I'm engaged or married, or if I have children.

SIMONE: Not at all. But maybe so. After all, you're the same age as my daughter's daughter.

AXELLE: Why don't you just say, 'You're my granddaughter's age'?

SIMONE: I don't know. Maybe because the word *granddaughter* always seems to imply a very young child?

AXELLE: Is she the person you were supposed to meet?

SIMONE: Yes. I haven't seen her in fifteen years.

AXELLE: Are you sure it's worth it?

SIMONE: What do you mean?

AXELLE: I don't know. For example, she may disappoint you. Maybe she's on drugs, or a young offender, ignorant. Selfish. She may even be crazy.

SIMONE: It never occurred to me.

AXELLE: Where do parents get the idea their children are going to be good-looking, smart and, especially, nice to them? I find this a bit sick.

SIMONE: Sick?

AXELLE: Vulgar, if you prefer. Thinking your child will be the same as you shows a lack of awareness of the laws of heredity. It's also vulgar to aspire to eternal youth. Sorry ... I'm a geneticist. To answer your question: yes, I like jazz. When I was little, my father and mother often took me to the homes of musician friends. We were like a big family gathered around the music of Duke Ellington. Each couple would bring their children and for us it was a party. There was a little boy who was fascinated by Dungeons and Dragons. He read all the time. And there was a girl named Ella who liked to talk about the Aztecs. Later, after my father left, my mother made me take piano lessons. I liked music, but I couldn't play. Every time my fingers touched the keys, I'd see the bones of my hands. My hands on the keyboard always gave me the impression somebody else was playing, not me. After a few minutes I'd stop and cry. The teacher forced me to continue. I did the best I could. Intrigued, frightened and fascinated by the movement of what I called 'my soul gone wild' on the keyboard.

SIMONE: You're so young, yet you talk like somebody who's had a full life.

AXELLE: Or who remembers everything. Which isn't the same thing.

SIMONE: At your age I was already a mother. I was dreaming of travelling and museums. As a child I had an uncle who was a Jesuit missionary, and every time he came home, his words carried my cousins and me to increasingly fascinating places. In Shanghai, Manila, Abidjan and Abyssinia, we ate rice, died of thirst, walked in the dust and excrement among goats, dogs and lepers. We trudged through thick forests until suddenly temples and pagodas changed into elephants, cobras, tigers and lions. He also talked about feminine curves he called caryatids, canephoras or bilobate rose windows. I told many of these stories again when my daughter was born, and telling them allowed me to travel over and over.

CARLA: You should have told me a bit more about Simone Lambert. I find her interesting as a woman and as a character. She's a wounded woman. I like wounded women. They're alive, moving. I'm not being ironic. It's true. They move me. A wounded woman there in front of you, existing, moving her lips in the name of life, deeply disturbs me. It's like an abyss of transparency and mystery. In college, in Regina, there was a girl with indescribably blue eyes working in the cafeteria. Her job was to place the desserts on the counter. Every day we'd file past her, kept apart by rows of rice pudding, crème caramel and fruit salad. I would dive into her eyes, swim vigorously, go down to the bottom of an unfathomable sadness, then come back up to the surface, feeling relieved that such sadness wasn't mine. For two years I thought I was in love with this girl. Her sadness turned me on. Wounds, scars, tattoos – I can't help it, I do indeed have a thing for skin graffiti.

NARRATOR: Do you have a tattoo?

CARLA: No.

NARRATOR: I do. There. (*She points to her heart.*) Skin is thin in that area. It's painful. But that's what a tattoo is about, isn't it? To not suffer anywhere else but your skin. To circumscribe the pain in a specific place. To not forget that it's *that*.

CARLA: Is it recent?

NARRATOR: Yes. (*silence*) I got it after my mother died. Probably to signal that the world was beginning all over again. It's the

166

only time I've ever wanted to imitate my mother. I probably belong to that generation of women who can say, 'My mother had a tattoo on her shoulder.' Mine had a blue lion that stared right at me throughout my childhood. Sixty years later, that lion had become a blurred and ridiculous beast on the flaccid skin of an old lady in the agony of her death.

CARLA: You said it.

NARRATOR: What?

CARLA: The word *agony,* which scares you so much and which you didn't want me to use because it grates your ears. A loaded word, with two others inside it: one, *go*, that makes you move forward, the other, *ago*, that forces you to look backward. When I was very young I started deconstructing words, messing around with their syllables, like when you shake a handbag until the last coin, the tiniest key, falls out. Falls at our young feet. Falls into our young gaze. Actually, you know, words have always scared me. Maybe that's why I fold and unfold them over on themselves, in myself. Maybe you're refusing to read my manuscript for the same reason. (*as though she's just made a discovery*) That's it: you're afraid of words too.

NARRATOR: (*embarrassed*) Don't be ridiculous. Anyway, not here, not now.

CARLA: Yes! Yes, you're afraid. And what's worse, you're too proud to admit something that, if you did admit it, would make you a heroine. The history of literature teaches us that we have to be afraid. Everybody is afraid. Everybody identifies with an author who's afraid. It's reassuring to know we're not alone, stuck in the middle of fear and distress. And so on until you understand that *I is someone else* is a hollow phrase that makes you an irresponsible being.

NARRATOR: I think I'm afraid of the conflicts hiding inside words. But words don't scare me. They give me a lot of pleasure. Fabrice had an exceptional way with them. Never natural. That's it, I like verbal fireworks. Okay, there, you win. The next time we get together, bring me your manuscript. I'll finally read that Chapter Five you've been pestering me about for all these weeks.

CARLA: Are you afraid or not?

NARRATOR: I'm afraid.

SIMONE: I think I'm going to give the go-ahead for the exhibition on ruins she (*nodding toward the narrator*) is proposing. How can we not be sensitive to what ruins represent today? Even in this field, things have changed. In bygone days, *ruins* meant what remains of a civilization, of a culture, of a reality. People could learn from ruins, rewind the thread of history back to the splendour and zenith of a civilization. People could dream around ruins. Dream, I mean *live* amid images, be borne by the idea that two thousand, four thousand years ago, life was throbbing in full colour, voice and movement. What will the ruins of our civilization look like? But first we'd need to know which civilization we're talking about. The civilization of humanism? Or of genomics and transgenics, which will turn us into mutants more conventional than three John-Paul IIs in one? Our ruins won't boil down to some debris and garbage left in the middle of mined and contaminated fields, a few cans, car skeletons and rusted hangars. Our ruins will be electromagnetic and radioactive. Does it annoy you when somebody my age tells you this?

AXELLE: It kills me. Yes, it deeply embarrasses me. It's as though you were announcing that the future won't look like the future.

SIMONE: (*uncomfortable*) Have you had time to visit the city?

AXELLE: Not yet, but tomorrow I hope to find a moment between two panel discussions.

SIMONE: Come and see me at the Museum of Civilization.

AXELLE: I don't really *do* museums, as they say. When I was a child, my grandmother often took me to the museum. She'd explain everything I saw and especially what I didn't see, with the patience of an angel. She had a collection of T-shirts from every museum in the world. She brought me some in all colours, with typefaces in Arabic, Chinese, Greek, Russian. My mother used to say she spoiled me, that she took up too much space everywhere she went. How many times, on a bus or in a restaurant, did I yell, 'Grandmother, you're taking up too much space'? She'd laugh, point to the space between us and say, 'See, that's not true.' She never understood why I said that. Nor did I, actually. It had become a habit, a game. It's only now, as I'm telling you this story, that my mother's words are making sense.

SIMONE: (*trying to hide her emotions*) There are other museums obviously. Anyway, you'll see. But tell me exactly what your work is.

AXELLE: I do research. I spend a large part of my days in the lab, the other part in meetings or writing articles. My research is confidential. Let's just say I'm studying what's called the living world.

SIMONE: (*still very emotional*) You mustn't be short of friends.

AXELLE: I don't go out much. I go dancing once a week. I work out regularly in a gym. I sleep eight hours. I never eat more than two thousand calories a day. I never watch TV. My computer screen is quite enough to ruin my eyesight. That's all. Evenings before going to sleep I recite a poem to myself. It's a habit from when my mother and I lived in the South. My mother knew several poets down there. Some of them used to come to the house with their wives and children. Sometimes the kids were asked to recite a poem. I was always asked for 'A Little Sonata to the Moon and the Iroquois.' One day, my mother asked me to recite a poem by Octavio Paz in front of Octavio Paz. He was sitting in a big armchair smiling at me. Behind his head was the shelf where my mother kept her hibiscus. I pronounced every word of the poem with meticulous care, looking straight ahead at the red flowers and the poet's grey hair blurring my gaze.

You know, my mother wasn't perfect, but she did transmit her love of poetry to me, which exonerates her from all blame. All the poems I know I carry inside me, like my mother's memory. I learned them all by heart when she was still living by my side.

> *Cuánto pesa un ojo en la balanza?*
> *Cuánto mide un sueño entre dos parpados?*
> *Cuánto pesa en tus manos un ojo cerrado,*
> *Un ojo de muerto y un ojo pelado?*
> — Homero Aridjis

CARLA: I wonder what creates fear even when there's no clear and present danger. People are always saying they're afraid of this and that, of the wind, of snakes, of old flames. It's clear and specific. When we say, 'I'm afraid of being cold, I'm afraid of not being able to breathe,' it's because we're evaluating a risk or, rather, because we're afraid the evaluation we're making is wrong. But being afraid of writing, that must be like being afraid of living, being afraid of oneself, fearing life itself.

NARRATOR: Maybe we're afraid all the time, without realizing it. Afraid of dying or afraid of wanting to die. But now is not a good time to discuss this. I want to talk to Simone Lambert some more about my exhibition.

CARLA: At this hour?

NARRATOR: Yes, it's now or never. It's important. I'm running around in circles with this project. You should see my apartment. Now that would scare you. I mean, you'd be scared of the person living there.

CARLA: I've seen messy apartments before.

NARRATOR: My apartment looks like the apartments of people who have that sickness, you know, that stops them from throwing out things that have become useless, that forces them to save empty matchbooks, toothpaste tubes, liquor bottles, chewing-gum packets. But they also stock up on newspapers, magazines, calendars, even if it means dying of asphyxiation amid their documents. I've become a dangerous collector.

CARLA: Dangerous? Well, you're not collecting boa constrictors, revolvers or deadly poisons, are you?

NARRATOR: Worse. I collect images of ruins, blind spots of civilization. I surround myself with debris, relics of ancient glories, old style manuals. I sit at my work table for hours on end, captivated by a pattern, by a suspicious relief. Do you realize: every day, I have to deal with remnants of desire, irrefutable evidence of violence, of destruction or of wear. My task is to make sure people remember well how life was before us. 'The ideas ruins awaken in me are grand. Everything comes to nothing, everything perishes, everything passes, only the world remains, only time endures. How old the world is!' said Diderot. Well, I invest ruins with power, with such power to question that part of the reality surrounding me loses its meaning. I'm fascinated by which part of a dream, of a civilization, collapses, just like an architect surely wonders what will collapse first in a church, a library, a hospital or a stadium. What are the first signs of the decay of a setting?

CARLA: This way you have of never talking about yourself is very strange. You're always creating questions and emergencies that seem so remote from daily life, from your life, from Québecois reality.

NARRATOR: That's fine by me. I'm interested in ruins because I'm interested in time, in this jaw open on the cosmos and on our genes. In any case, you rarely give me the opportunity to talk about intimate things which, as you see it, form the fine fabric of creation. For you, each one of our encounters will have been an outlet. But for me it will have been more of an exercise in listening, though I shan't deny the pleasure derived from it –

173

(*silence*) a sensory pleasure fraught with intensity. Come, let's join Simone and the young woman.

CARLA: Good idea. I'm going to invite them to my room for a drink. That way it'll be easier for you to talk with Simone. And you can take the copy of Chapter Five. (*looking at the two women*) They seem to be getting along well.

CARLA CARLSON'S ROOM

All hotel rooms have angles. Dead angles such as closets, the bathroom door, the space under the bed. Living angles: windows, mirrors, chairs and armchairs where one can always read or watch dust particles move through the air like quicksilver confetti. Carla Carlson's room is partly occupied by twin beds. On one of them, books, file folders, a camera and an umbrella. One of the walls, the one with the first light switch encountered by fingers after opening the door to the room, is papered with typewritten pages streaked here and there with deletions in red ink. Others have only a handwritten title. There is a dresser with a large mirror which Carla has used to photograph herself from all angles and under different lighting. For in the morning, when the whiteness of day filters through the muslin curtains, Carla enters an altered state of perception that makes her want to commit to memory some of the dead angles. In the afternoon, if it rains or when the sky is heavy and a light grey pearls the room's atmosphere, she interrupts her writing to photograph what she calls the wild aura of the price to be paid for writing. As for the nighttime lighting, it is of an almost Mexican sunflower yellow and appears only when Carla returns to her room following long conversations with that woman who works at the Museum of Civilization and whom she met when she first arrived in Québec City. Since then, they meet in the hotel bar to listen to a bit of jazz and regale each other with stories, facts and complex arguments which, Carla admits, move her manuscript forward. Be that as it may, the room as setting is sometimes filled with accents and foreign words which take on such fictional airs that they are transformed under the effect of diaereses, circumflex and acute accents, each one giving the impression of closing in around meaning, a real slip knot. Such is the case of hotel room settings where, time and again, objects appear like visual refuges put at our disposal to take better advantage of the characters and the mystery surrounding them. And so, should we say that each setting serves to draw us closer to our loved ones, who roam in our memories like characters or like deer gorged on vertigo and horizon? The room where the four women seen in the Hotel Clarendon bar between ten and quarter past midnight will soon gather is spacious. The dresser in front of the twin beds has a mirror which can also work as a screen during the perform-ance. Simone and Axelle are each seated on one of the beds and looking in the direction of the mirror-screen. Throughout the following scenes, they are seen from behind but their faces are visible if the audience looks up at the screen. Carla and the narrator come and go in the room. Sometimes they sit side by side looking at the audience. Typewritten pages are taped to the wall adjoining the main hallway of this hotel floor. During the performance, the actresses will be seen or heard reading from them.

For years I lived with fragments of civilization in my hands, russet dust, old ochre sand frolicking on my fingertips. My life is peopled with ancient civilizations I've learned to know, to love, to classify, to assemble, to embed in my thoughts so as to give them a look of truth. Now this scares me. On the sites, my life was radically split into black and white. White light that turned blue into lilac, yellow into gold dust. Black of night fallen like a rare petal upon our shoulders. Night. Sleep. The sleep of insects while night became sombre-eyed and an incalculable number of naïve questions lingered around the lips. I persisted among the stones with questions that set bones afire. On certain days, I confess, I lost contact with the individuals coming and going around me, gathering their strength and their tools. I thought that, after all, nothing is absolutely true, and this made me feel good.

CARLA

Ah! Simone, it pleases me when you get to the heart of the matter like this. Alas! We're losing the habit of it. Too many distractions. Too much decency too. And isn't a sense of decency required to live in society?

NARRATOR

The apparent simplicity of the contemporary reflex urging us to get things done shortly and sweetly doesn't excuse us from understanding. (*turning to Axelle*) May I call you by your given name?

CARLA

We have to distinguish between the lust for life and the lust to exist. The difference is similar to the one we've set up between fiction and reality. Yet, in either case, a doubt always exists as to whether it's our imagination or our very familiar body that misleads us about our hunger. In my novel, there's a parrot-character present at Descartes's death. The parrot is playful. You should hear him: 'Papa struts his stuff Papa puffs it up old hound dog belching and leching on the Prairies old Papa old hound-dog-eared pappy loves flirty hotties.' I'd like to make Descartes stark-raving mad but he has to stay focused on himself disguised as his own character and to speak seductive sentences about the lust for life that gives us material for madness.

AXELLE

My mother often ranted madly out of the blue. If she asked me a question and I didn't respond the next second, she'd start a long monologue about precious time not to be wasted. During her rants, she'd accuse all societies of imprisoning women's time in little silver rings or in heavy dusty drawers which, afterwards, they had to sand smooth from the inside. When there was no free time left around women, my mother said society swallowed them up once and for all and that we never heard about them anymore. She often said, 'We have very little time left,' or 'Hurry up, the storm is coming.' 'Hurry up and be successful.'

SIMONE

At least she talked to you. I never had much time for my daughter.

NARRATOR

You mustn't say that. Mothers, alas, always have too much time for their daughters, and even when they don't, the daughters feel it's too much.

SIMONE

What are you talking about?

180

NARRATOR

I simply wanted to say that mothers are omnipresent and that many daughters could do without.

CARLA

Legend has it otherwise. Quite the contrary. More often than not, daughters have been orphaned, abandoned or rejected.

NARRATOR

Daughters don't know what they want. Too much is not enough and not enough is like absence.

AXELLE

Soon we won't be able to tell the difference between womb-mother and gene-mother. Mother by instinct and mother by abandonment. Little old-boned mother and big fat mother of sorrow. You all come from another time. You think in words loaded with fervour. But fervour isn't very effective when compared to a perfect equation, a well-drawn genetic map, a precise number.

CARLA

Excuse me, but fervour is rather exciting!

AXELLE

Fervour amounts to nothing. Or let's just say that it simply feeds old remnants of pain.

CARLA

Pain leads to thinking and thinking isn't nothing. It's actually rather a privilege to be able to think.

AXELLE

Thinking should be as easy as fucking. Well, I mean, if fucking were simple.

NARRATOR

Everybody ruminates, mentally toys with topics. It's called thinking *au naturel*. There's a prejudice according to which only people who think abstract thoughts think for real, but I believe that thinking also means hanging around among words, images and ideas. All told, thinking may be reaching a conclusion at the right moment in a rumination. Do we think well naturally or does thinking well imply an effort, that we accept getting lost, retracing our steps, hitting the wall, a knot, that we take the time to unscramble faulty reasoning, to erase a thought that's greedy or petty?

AXELLE

What a strange night! Today should be an important day for me. I so wanted not to be disappointed. I wanted her in front of me, that woman who could have explained my mother to me. Why do we say *grandmother* instead of *my mother's mother*?

NARRATOR

It makes it possible to better frame the possessive, to put it where it matters most to you. Also, when you say *my mother's mother*, you're entering the realm of emotional genealogy which, it's well-known, is undermined by tiredness, by dailiness and especially by that nervous and complex anxiety that enters any possessive relationship. You can't say, 'I was walking hand in hand with my mother's mother.' That's too many people on the sidewalk at the same time.

SIMONE

I fail to see why you persist in making such a natural filial bond so horribly complicated.

NARRATOR

I'm suggesting paths to understand a bond that, though natural, is nonetheless dangerous.

(moving closer to the wall)

Last: say *last* without bursting out laughing, maybe that's what Descartes meant when he crossed the inner courtyard to get from his apartment to Queen Christina's. *To last*, now there's a verb my naïve papa sometimes confused with *to endure*. Misery, no! Not *misery* like many of the characters often written into our literature. No. Not *misery*. *Enduring* time. Time that passed coldly over our buffalo shoulders attracted by the horizon and the vast sudden emptiness of the badlands. *Enduring* by sharpening one's everyday knife, pressing up against trees once night has fallen and dreaming of cities to the south and ancestors to the north, even further north, there where my papa believed his mother's soul may still be wandering. *(gesturing to the pages taped to the wall)* This is my novel – read it if you like. I'm almost done. One more week and I'm going home to Saskatoon. I've started dreaming about the old silence that surrounded the house of my childhood. And I've been having dreams of buffalo for the last two days. I can hear the terrifying sound of their furious race toward the edge of the cliff they leap from, flinging themselves into the abyss, and piling up one on top of the other, horns and body parts mixed with blood, dust and the russet grass, one blurry blade of grass swaying in front of their great almost-dead almost-blind eyes, their great eyes led astray by the void and the coldness of the horizon.

Why do you say *my naïve papa*?

Because he was sweet and easily let himself be tied up like a doll when we played cowboys. He was always ready to die, no matter how my story started or ended. He was ready. Just like that, standing straight up in the wind. He'd say, 'Okay, girl, it's time for me to die.' So then I'd get on my horse and join up with

Queen Christina. Sometimes I had to make the return trip several times between Stockholm and Rome. At other times I'd go directly to Rome, entering via the Appian Way, then, without any transitional scene, I'd find myself in the queen's arms again. We'd share a long kiss behind a screen. Somebody would bring us figs and *fragole*. We'd kiss one last time and then I'd say, 'Okay, girl, it's time for me to go,' and I'd come back to the rape field I'd left just a few minutes before.

SIMONE

I think I'm going to go now.

NARRATOR

No, Simone, stay. I'll take you home later. I know this may not be the right time but …

SIMONE

Right, now is not the time. Axelle, I'd like you to take me home. We need to talk.

AXELLE

I can't see what about. I have only one subject of conversation in mind and I don't think you can help me out.

SIMONE

That's good. I have only one person in mind and I believe you can talk to me about her.

AXELLE

(*moves closer to the wall and reads the following passage*)
'I imagine it takes joy about all things to rush into time and let it close in around us. Yes, one must doubtless allow time to swallow silence and the multiform narratives that surround us like a hedge of roses.'

FADE OUT.

    FADE IN.

The screen switches on, showing close-ups of Axelle's and Simone's faces. Both are focused as though watching a show, a movie. If the technology exists, I'd like it if it were possible to work on the faces live so as to emphasize the features the actresses can't work on. This way, their exchange would create a very strange impression. We enter the thick of the conversation they would have had had they met in the restaurant.

SIMONE

It's a truly great day. I'd almost resigned myself to not seeing you again. If you only knew all the imaginary portraits of you I've conjured in my mind.

AXELLE

I was looking forward to seeing you. I'd have liked to come sooner but, you know, I work hard.

SIMONE

I know.

AXELLE

It's as though everywhere I go I'm just a passerby. (*Silence. Church bells can be heard.*) The night before she disappeared, Mother had insomnia. I heard her walking around the house and talking on the phone. I fell asleep. When I woke up the next day, the house was quiet. Breakfast was visibly set out on the yellow and agave-green placemat. Only one setting. I sat at my usual place. I gulped down a glass of orange juice. A trickle of juice ran down my neck. There was an envelope in the bread-basket. I took it. It was Mother's writing. It contained a hundred American dollars and the address and phone number of a family of friends who lived close by and who sometimes invited us to spend the weekend in Tepoztlán. Maybe Mother wrote to you or told you about them. The father is a great pianist and the mother an important businesswoman whose husband used to say, 'Without her, workers would be jobless, the jobless would be poor, the poor would be slaves, and slaves would be corpses.' That morning I ate everything on the table. I called the family-planning centre where Mother worked. She wasn't there. I sat in the garden, a tiny garden where she grew basil and chives. The neighbour's dog was barking. It was a gorgeous day, blue everywhere. People think a ten-year-old child is unable to think and to really want. Something. At that very moment, more than anything, I wanted my mother, her rough and busy gestures, her worried look, her blue eyes which, even when she was angry, always seemed soft. Looking in her eyes was like going to the movies. I always tried to do it as long as possible. Children rarely look their parents in the eye, but I always looked at my mother right in the eye. Eventually she'd laugh and say, 'Hurry up and look at me, we're leaving.' When I looked at her I felt like I was honouring her and getting closer to her dreams, to her real dreams. At night I sometimes heard her screaming or talking in a halting voice.

That day, the police came with Mr. Morelos and his oldest daughter, Liliana. They searched the house. I asked them what they were looking for and they said papers. Liliana helped me fill a suitcase with everything I loved and wanted to take with me. I took a picture of Mother, my microscope, books, a poster of Frida Kahlo which Liliana rolled up with a flick of her wrists. We weren't going far. The Moreloses lived a few streets away. Days went by. Months. The Morelos family probably tried to reach you, but there was nobody at your Montréal address. My father was nowhere to be found. So they decided to adopt me. Two years later they settled in New York, a large apartment close to Columbia University. I had a big room. We lived on the fifteenth floor. A major silence reigned in which I strove to detect the city's soundtrack – it produced a breathing sound I'd call nothing short of suave. Which made the whole family laugh at mealtimes. I was sent to Bard College. Then I studied genetics at Princeton.

SIMONE

Shortly after you left for Mexico, I was offered a job as director of a new museum here in Québec City. I've been living in the same place since then. I like it. The river's presence makes me happy. Like you, I work non-stop. Nobody has forced me to retire yet. I travel a lot, but with less and less enthusiasm. I haven't done any fieldwork for ages. So I'm left with museum hallways and big exhibition rooms. Not a day has gone by that I haven't thought about Lorraine and you. *To disappear*. As if I were destined to live among traces, evidence of the past, to preserve the memory of what once existed in its full glory. Seeing you here in front of me leaves me at a loss. You look like Lorraine. I'm moved to the very foundation of (*she looks for the words*) my silence.

AXELLE

That's a strange expression.

SIMONE

Maybe so. How else can one express the essential things that run through our relationship to time and continuity, our little lonesome-beast murmurings as we roam the cosmos?

AXELLE

The silence of our cells or the silence surrounding our cells? The sound effect of the soul, as my gene-manipulating colleagues put it.

A friend of mine just died, alone, in the deepest dark Turkish night. Alone, far away, like your mother, one day in May, just when the days are growing longer and when the idea of life takes full-bodied shape, gorges us with pleasure and the pride of being alive.

AXELLE

(suddenly and violently)

My mother isn't dead. She disappeared. It's not the same thing. What did you do to my mother for her to hate you so much?

FADE OUT.
     FADE IN.

CARLA

None of the books I consulted say anything at all about why
Queen Christina chose to leave for Rome. I've spent my whole
life as a novelist pondering what motives hide behind gestures
and decisions of abandonment and departure. What obscure
motive brings me to Québec City to finish each one of my
novels? Of course I've uncovered some derisory answers. For a
time I believed it was because of the Louis Riel poem 'O Québec'
which my little French-Canadian friends used to recite during
our two-month vacations. In it, Riel begs the province of Québec
to not forget the Métis of Manitoba the way France forgot
Québec after her defeat. A terrible poem, but the 'O Québec'
resonated in me like a word, a place full of mysteries where
everything seemed possible. I like writing to gain some time
over absurdity. I write to reconnect with the imagery of my
wanderings along the South Saskatchewan River. In French, we
say *rivière aux amélanchiers*, that is, Saskatoon Berry River.
Bottom line, I think well only when I'm deflecting beings from
their usual functions and assigning them new roles in the story.
The impulse to fiction is surely worth a gram of coke to erase all
traces of the absurd.

NARRATOR

Oh, that old word.

CARLA

Words age, but they are never old. You'd have to be a moron
to not acknowledge the absurd. A moron or a heavy consumer
of futile spectacles. 'The absence of change is,' they say, 'the

189

apparent characterictic of the absurd.' Indeed, if we agree that the St. Bartholomew's Day massacre equals the Rwanda massacre, and that the Massacre of the Innocents ranks with the one at Shatila, it's because the word *absurd* is still potent.

NARRATOR

Ionesco believed that people had become walls for one another. My impression is more that we've become a constant wall of sound, changing, stifling and fascinating one another – background noise that runs us into the ground.

CARLA

What was your mother like, Axelle?

Axelle does not reply immediately.

CARLA

(*softly*) What was she like?

AXELLE

I don't really know. She was always occupied, preoccupied, (*looking at Simone*) a woman whose life centred on her mother, (*pointing toward Simone*) whose life was miserable because of you. Don't worry, she wouldn't reproach you for anything in particular. It's just that you were there, everywhere, like a shadow, a ghost, an inexplicable threat. And this despite the dream-come-true evenings she told me about. You took her to the most prestigious museums, you had the great libraries of the world opened for her so the two of you could spend a few hours admiring rare documents, parchments, silks, incunabula.

NARRATOR

A mother who educates her daughter deserves the greatest respect. All daughters dream of a mother who could teach them the world, reality, and also make them dream.

SIMONE

All around us the world is a flavour to be transmitted. Mothers have forever transmitted, often unbeknownst to themselves, a kind of future.

AXELLE

We can't talk about the future in the same way anymore. Let's push this to the backs of our minds once and for all.

CARLA

The future is always composed of what we're given to toy with as children. My mother gave me Descartes and Queen Christina. Unawares, my father left me a gift for lassoing characters. As for school, it offered me names like Sir John Macdonald and General Middleton but I never knew what to do with them. I preferred playing with the Latin and French words the Laramée sisters taught me on Sunday afternoons. And you, Axelle, what were you given to play with for your life and for this future you're trying to warn us against?

AXELLE

My mother left me the words *justice, freedom, transgression*. And *work*. Only words. She left me only words.

SIMONE

Lorraine hated work, discipline. She loved adventure, risk, stories about witches and community life. She mixed everything up with her ideas about revolution, Zen, herbs and cayenne pepper.

AXELLE

My mother was a wise and knowledgeable woman. Maybe too sensitive – no, touchy, like proud people are. She was like electrical current going through the house. The silence of the house. She demanded an impeccable silence of me: reading / writing /

reflecting, those were the activities on offer. It was only once I was living with the Moreloses that I started laughing and masturbating. (*silence*) Yes, masturbating – an action verb that puts you back in touch with yourself and with the faculty of imagining improbable, unmentionable scenes, sometimes grotesque. At Princeton, girls masturbated a lot before exams. Some evenings it was contagious.

Long silence.

FADE OUT.

FADE IN.

*The four women are sitting around a card table. They have ordered
food, and on the table there is a bottle of champagne as well as olives
and smoked salmon.*

CARLA

I'm happy you decided to stay. There comes a moment during
the night when there's no going back nor any flight forward.
You simply have to stay up. Just stay and embody yourself in the
contours of the night, awaiting the contours of dawn.

SIMONE

You were right to insist that I stay. I feel better. Bon appétit. It
has always fascinated me to think that exquisite matter such as
caviar, olives, truffles, cheese, raspberries, the champagne we're
about to rapturously drink are transformed in just a few hours
into matter ... let's say ... not so noble. It's almost a miracle that
so many dreams, stories and work are contained in the foods
that end up on our plates and in our mouths! As soon as I speak
or see the word *olive*, I'm transported to Sicily or Andalusia. I
have a siesta, I stop at a terrace for some lemonade. Time passes.

CARLA

Keso, fransbröd och brännvin.

NARRATOR

Prozac, DHEA, Viagra, testosterone, growth hormones. You are
what you eat, oh my beautiful transgenic one. My beloved, my
wild species among all species.

193

What exhausts me in the novel is having to take countless phrasal detours to succeed at describing what my eyes – wild with joy or with pain – can see. Endless detours to successfully translate *I love you*. Come into my arms. Forgive me. Never again. Again and again. A real digestive system which, unlike our own, would be able to produce something new from the raw material of impressions and sensations.

AXELLE

It mustn't be easy, being a character.

CARLA

No. *Character*, meaning pretending to be real –

NARRATOR

– and to suffer, but what for?

AXELLE

Suffering for real while pretending to suffer adequately.

CARLA

Like an actress, then? But an actress isn't a character. She's often me.

SIMONE

A long time ago I knew an actress named Alma Longsong. She was a friend of the great Egyptian singer Oum Kalsoum, whose voice made the whole Middle East vibrate. I met them in a café in Cairo. I was working at Abu-Simbel at the time and every month I'd go to Cairo to meet civil servants and sign papers. Whenever it was possible, I'd go to the theatre to see Alma onstage; she had a perfect face. You know, it's unusual to hear about a woman with a perfect face who is capable of speaking about our notions not of the beautiful face but of the perfect face. Her theory was simple and thrilling. The perfect face should never be imagined based on the *O* but should have a *U* as centre of attraction. The *O*, she said, attracted too much imagination to the top of the skull and thus forced the beholder to juxtapose the skull and the perfection of the face.

AXELLE

One could just as easily argue the exact opposite. That the *U* is insufficient when it comes to translating the whole face and so, as long as the top of the skull is missing, the essential is missing.

SIMONE

Exactly. That's how the theory was simple. And thrilling it was, because it permitted thinking about the rare perfect faces of women which, as far back as one can recall, have been the basis of a bank of images of transcendence.

AXELLE

My mother's face was perfect. Since she disappeared it has never stopped haunting me. I don't know if it's because of its perfection or because I don't know what became of it. What was it, age or death, that overcame her forehead, her tender cheeks, her mouth capable of the sharpest sounds and the cruellest sentences?

NARRATOR

(who has already stood up and walked over to the wall,
reads this passage from the novel)

'Daily living is an achievement. I'm surrounded by cries, by long laments and a wild and shy energy that transforms both the world and my mother's silence into fiction, into an outgrowth of life, a nameless virtuality … Without my mother's silence I am left wide open to the static noise that amplifies the coward in each one of us.'

195

FADE OUT.

    FADE IN.

SIMONE

The extreme solitude of women.

CARLA

Do you mean yours or ours?

SIMONE

I mean the extreme solitude of women like a resonating body that amplifies the fear and sorrow of smooth-sobbing women. Women who say to themselves every day, 'It makes no sense to have been born in this godforsaken place without water or electricity but loaded with tradition and religion, which put the noose around our neck. It makes no sense that my life be shrivelled up stupid because of men's weakness for violence and their learned contempt for us.'

AXELLE

You know, part of the solitude is in illness, in the body's powerlessness to move toward others, to circulate among others.

CARLA
(in an ironic tone)
And where, in your opinion, can this other be found?

SIMONE
(as if in support of what Axelle has said)
The other isn't hiding. She's feeding the first one. She's constantly manufacturing silence and it's up to each and every one of us to make the most of it.

And what can be made from silence?

Silence contains everything required to live happily.

For example?

From silence streams everything we call *art*, including the art of living. Imagining without silence or without the constraint of silence would be unthinkable. Silence contains all the keys of our programming. The pleasure we take in respecting the constraints that keep happiness at bay constitutes our art of living – in short, a way of living by keeping open a window that would look out onto a wall. Some days the wall is opaque, sombre and repulsive, other days its transparency is an invitation to scale it or to enjoy its luminosity. The wall doesn't protect us, nor does it keep us from something that would be attractive. The wall is a desirable illusion that keeps us alive, in a state of vigilance amid old sentences that make us dream and die all in the same breath. Today science claims that one day we'll be able to go through that wall and so put an end to the noxious attraction we've always had for excesses, the very ones that allowed us to nurture our fascination for the wall and to sometimes find, in its transparency, the fertile figures of our age-old nostalgia.

I prefer to work on our little memories sweetened with a flavour like that of jam, the aroma of coffee, the perfume on women's necks or those lovely blue soap bubbles that do so-soft things to our skin when we sink into the tub. I prefer to work on the idea that each one of us is inventing a new fate for humanity, with or without the melancholy of summer evenings.

We know so much about our species and so little about women. And yet, see, I was going to say that we're prepared to deprive ourselves of freedom in order to increase our knowledge. I wonder what will happen if we continue to spy on the species in the infinite smallness of our cries, hoping for an explanation that would justify an impending immortality. Soon, looking at it close up, we'll be able to detect our shadow, our double, our pure-fiction *I* busy manipulating our very own genes. Axelle, don't you think you do terribly dangerous work?

AXELLE

'My only fear is the fear of not dying.' I swear it on my mother's body.

CARLA

On Sundays I used to go to the cemetery with the little Laramée girls, who taught me Latin and a few words of French. We'd walk among the graves talking like adults. We'd all bring a sandwich and at about eleven-thirty, when the sun was searing our scalps, seek shelter by a tombstone in the shade. The sisters would sit in front of me. Anne would put on her glasses. I'd look at Margot's knees, which always had bruises on them, blue, bloody or pinkish. I stared obstinately at her kneecaps and mechanically repeated after her lines from *The Aeneid*. Butterflies, flies and mosquitoes flew around us. We always chose a grave with fresh flowers. Sometimes there was still a bit of dew on a petal. Then the sisters would force me to decline *rosa rosae* for a rose, you know … Then, after eating, we'd have long discussions about the diffuse happiness which the sight of the petal had triggered in us.

SIMONE

I never got used to the idea of being called *Mother*. Lorraine sometimes brought over little friends who said *Mom* and *Mum*.

When Lorraine said *my mother*, I thought she was talking about somebody else, a nun maybe. To my ears, *my mother* has always sounded like the screech of a seagull. One day I asked her to call me Simone. That's when she started to say, 'I'm Simone's daughter but I'm not my mother's daughter anymore.'

AXELLE

I always called her *Mother*. I don't think I'm ever going to have children. I don't understand why grandmothers always seem to have a greater love of life than mothers do. I don't understand why things seem to exist only if they quiver under our eyes and ravage the heart before impaling themselves on our thoughts.

SIMONE

Carla, you write novels, so what's the point of rediscovering one's childhood? I don't know why but I always get the impression that novelists write to rediscover the few rare moments of a terrific and full joy experienced amid their close relations or, on the contrary, the better to flee those same relations and their conformity. Basically, maybe we do the same job. We go on digs and then, each in her own way, expose the remains, debris and fragments of a great whole that once existed, which may be nothing more and nothing less than a huge burst of laughter, a nameless euphoria, a pain so raw that we have to make sense of it.

CARLA

I don't know. Sometimes I tell myself it's enough just to not forget. At other times I think there are new things to be understood by looking at people, and that if we describe their hair or their mouths, it'll be easier to love them or to make them speak.

SIMONE

Have you noticed that grandmothers never talk about themselves? They're always mysterious, ensconced in the grandchildren's vague memory. There they are, old, tired, bony or fat, shifting their decrepit flesh around under the children's valiant affectionate gaze. They are maternal or paternal and quite naturally they change into characters from books, from which they never exit. Only once they've been relocated in books does collective memory become interested in grandmothers. Then, once again, it classifies them by generations according to wars, famines and inventions which will in turn have scared them, pleased them or amused them: the car, the airplane, moving pictures, the radio, the pill, ATMs, the Internet.

NARRATOR

Have you noticed also how intensity always makes things happen, as if tomorrow kept reappearing like an angry torrent sweeping death and the past in its path? I always imagine myself walking with a solution in mind for everything that's alive. When I go to the museum or the market, everything becomes terribly present, a present that erases my every step. Sometimes I stop on Dufferin Terrace, astonished by the violet wind which, blowing from all sides, sates my desire for powerful sensations. I notice how readily the sad lads abandon themselves to the wind's violent arms. I notice how much being alive matters. We don't notice enough how, in spite of everything, life organizes itself so as not to fail us.

AXELLE

It may be better that way. I don't know. I work at refashioning the elements of life already programmed by nature. I quite like the idea of producing fragments of time, tiny kaleidoscopes that make the eye unfit to detect death. It's ridiculous. It's as though science is trendy because it attempts to make humanity lose its alphabet, its books of origins, its habits of the past and of ancestral solidarity. Every day I work on the immortality of my peers and I miss death.

NARRATOR

What are you talking about?

AXELLE

I'm talking about my little manipulations, thanks to which, in principle, dying will no longer be an *idée fixe*.

SIMONE

How so?

AXELLE

Change, old lady! (*They all turn toward Axelle with astonishment.*) I work on change. I ...

CARLA

The only valid changes stem from fiction.

A half-light slowly settles onto the stage/scene.

CARLA

Sometimes in the novels of yesteryear we read that people would let darkness softly enter a large room in the house while each person watched, be it the mother sitting, reading or sewing, or the brother wrestling with a younger sibling, or the father poring over an accounts ledger. Sometimes we read that the night is tender, that the room's half-light is where the sense of values stirs and that at the very back of memory, something like a pleasing vision, a brief conviction, suddenly lights up words with a wide and wacky meaning which life, afterwards, makes sure to emphasize amid colours, bruises and caresses. I often write the same scene where I'm with my mother, seated on the large veranda surrounding the house which was itself surrounded by fields and the horizon. When I work on this scene, I sometimes add a little falling rain, I hear it clattering on the white pebbles all around the garden in front of our house.

I also bring in the chirping of sparrows, the cawing of a crow. There are never any trees. I disallow myself trees and the description of their foliage; the idea that somebody could hang themselves or be lynched from the branches scares me too much. I would so love to write a scene where my mother and I are walking in a big North American city, but every time she starts talking as she walks, she brings me back to her little village of Rättvik by furtively tugging at the elbow of my red sweater where the wool is almost worn through. I hang there for a bit between the big city and the shores of Lake Siljan, while my mother is already dreaming of swimming and fairs. It was before the war, a war, there's always a war in my nights when people's souls start roaring. So then I sit on the verb *to be* and don't budge until my mother is done swimming, comes out of the water laughing before disappearing down a path where the smell of spruce will drug her with deep forest silence.

Novels must also talk about beasts. My papa, the lassoed man, did it very well during evenings of real solitude. He'd explain to my mother and me the damned stink of dogs found along the highways. Also the lamb's melancholy smell when the knife nears its throat. 'A smell can always be explained,' he'd say, 'and every emotion has one.' We had a horse, and some evenings Papa explained in what ways Kermess was remarkable and different from all the other horses. I remember his mane sometimes so soft to the touch you'd think you were galloping upon one of those clouds that zip over the Prairies like an arrow and whose existence takes on its full meaning as soon as the bluish grey that makes it visible starts to clear. *Papa could keep talking for hours when he spoke about horses.* There were numerous horse breeds: Akhal-Teke, Andalusian, Arabian, Barbary, Bashkir, Cherkessian, Criollo, Kabyle, Kirghiz, Marwari, Mongolian, Taki, Tatar, Yili. And when he talked about animals, you could imagine them parading, trotting, snorting, stamping or galloping until they were all lathered up. My habit of always having an animal living among my characters comes from my dad. No, it's not out of love but just because I understand my pain better if the animal sets the pace for my intentions.

Since I've been here I sometimes go to Rue Saint-Jean for a bit of taramasalata, a few black olives, bread and wine. On the way back I stop at Librairie Pantoute where I leaf through novels that make me want to write. I always buy at least one book so I can have the pleasure of a new novel in front of my stimuli-starved eyes. That's how, here and there, over the years, I purchased *Our Lady of the Flowers* by *(Carla signals with her hand that we need to guess the authors' names)* ——, *To the Lighthouse* by ——, *Paradiso* by ——, *L'obéissance* by ——, *Benito Cereno* by ——, *Le monde sur le flanc de la truite* by ——, *The Euguelion* by ——, *Running in the Family* by ——, *The Book of Promethea* by ——, *Heroine* by ——, *Childhood* by ——, *Tomorrow in the Battle Think on Me* by ——, *Molloy* by ——, *Crossing the River* by ——, *The Last of the African Kings* by ——, *Time Regained* by ——, *The First Man* by ——, *Fortuny* by ——, *The Little Girl Who Was Too Fond of Matches* by ——, *Death of Virgil* by ——, *Fontainebleau* by ——, *Le Soir du dinosaure* by ——, *Blue Eyes, Black Hair* by ——, *Un homme est une valse* by ——, *My Year in the No-Man's-Bay* by ——, *Les derniers jours de Noah Eisenbaum* by ——, *Pereira Declares* by ——, *Two Stories of Prague* by ——, *Next Episode* by ——, *Cobra* by ——, *La vie en prose* by ——, *The Lesbian Body* by ——, *Technique du marbre* by ——, *Mauve Desert* by ——, *Extinction* by ——, *The Opposing Shore* by ——, *Thérèse and Isabelle* by ——, *La déconvenue* by ——, *Meroë* by ——, *These Festive Nights* by ——, *In the Shadow of the Wind* by ——, *The Christmas Oratorio* by ——, *Le livre du devoir* by ——, *Nightwood* by ——, *The Tin Flute* by ——, *E. Luminata* by ——, *The Palace* by ——, *Parc Univers* by ——, *The Sea* by ——, *Microcosms* by ——, *Dios No Nos Quiere Contentos* by ——, *La nuit* by ——, *The Heart Is a Lonely Hunter* by ——, *The Swallower Swallowed* by ——, *Paulina 1880* by ——,

Memoria by ——, *Dust over the City* by ——, *Pylon* by ——, *A Universal History of Infamy* by ——, *The Autobiography of Alice B. Toklas* by ——, *Jos Connaissant* by ——, *The Life and Opinions of Tristram Shandy, Gentleman* by ——, *Nous parlerons comme on écrit* by ——, *Life: A User's Manual* by ——.

You see, I need books in order to come and go in the complex beauty of the world. (*Carla pretends to leave the room, then comes back with a bag of imaginary groceries which she deposits on the bed.*) Back in my hotel room I get rid of the objects cluttering the dresser and replace them with the olives, cheese and bread. I freshen the bed by plumping up the pillows so that the head is comfy. The cardinal's glare is always strange and threatening. The day I arrived in Québec City, I put a wooden parrot in front of the window. It's from a Mexican boutique, a nice bright yellow. The feathers on its neck form a green necklace and the tail feathers, royal blue, skim the line of the river and of the horizon in an uninterrupted movement. A set of strings helps keep it balanced in front of the curtain and every morning the parrot gives the impression of dawn and of a beautiful upside-down hourglass. Seated at the dressing table, I eat slowly. I can hear him walking in the room. The rustle of his robe against the edge of the bed mixes with the metallic sound of the aluminum foil packaging the olives and goat cheese. From time to time he groans and she rushes in, worried. It's raining outside, I know. A fine rain meets the windowpane. Down below, the asphalt shines no doubt like a slate mirror. Passersby walk fast. Behind me Helen hovers around the bed with white cloths and a basin. I can very clearly distinguish the face of the man lying on the bed. Unto himself he represents a whole genealogy of thinkers, new and old, who like him are about to blow out the candle forever burnt at both ends by life and death. The man's face is like the ones reproduced in the literature and history books the little Laramée sisters carried under their arms as though these were treasures more precious still than the olives and ham sandwiches prepared by our mothers.

She eats an olive and bites into her sandwich, looking around her. She sits on the bed like someone who usually reads before going to sleep. Simone is in an armchair, seated in the same pose as Pope Innocent X in Francis Bacon's painting. The narrator, standing, circles the bed as if she were looking for something in the drawers, under the bed, in the bathroom. The following lines will all be spoken by Carla, but they can be 'read' on the other actresses' lips as though the sound originated from them. Helen will be played by the narrator, the cardinal by Simone. During this time, Axelle is looking out the window.

This scene will be played in Latin.

CARTESIUS

Quam singulare cubiculum! Nescio ubinam sim. Quid latet citra velum illud exiguum? Veritas, forsitan? Ningitne? Ningitne, Helena? Perspicere jam non valeo arborem abietis, permagnam excelsamque arborem illam, quae me commovet quotiescumque in eam oculos conjicio, ac si per semetipsam magnus perspectus effici valeret. Noli a me digredi, Helena. Porrige mihi manum tuam. Tange frontem meam. Sine me postrema vice animo te effingere. Nudam. Vellem te nudatam sistere, postrema vice, ante iam caligantes oculos meos. Vellem adhuc scribere. Vellem te nudam esse. Vellem scribere, et te nudam ut primam auroram sistere.

CARDINALIS

Semper tamen umbra sinenda est ad nos appropiquare, nec eam reicere debemus. Postremam animi et corporis colluctationem umbra tantummodo efficere valet sinceram. Nullum postremum certamen cogitari potest absque umbra quadam super labias illorum pendente, qui aequales eorum amaverunt, et qui bene locuti sunt de anima, quae non videtur, et tamen est, utique est. Sed extant in nobis, amice mi, irae impetus qui etiam aestatis splendorem obtenebrare quaeunt. Extant, bene novi, irae tam ardentes quae nec cursu verborum, nec etiam idearum vel rationum cursu placari possunt.

Satis bene, heu, hoc novi.

CARDINALIS

Non vos alloquebar.

HELENA

(as if she hadn't heard)

Satis bene, heu, hoc novi. Ira est velut quidam dolor immanis, quo quondam se per vim insinuari valuit in artus nostros intimos, maxima desperatione delirantes. Et cum ira illa in intimis nervositatis nostrae sedem suam elegit, nihil potest nisi debiliores nos efficere, ac sensus desideriaque nostra decipere. Renate, noscere nunquam valebis quam intensa sit ira mea. De die in diem omni modo enitui te celare huius irae rationem, necnon horribiles illos tremores manuum et palpebrarum ab ea concitatos. Satis nunc habeo. Nunc loquar.

CARDINALIS

Nolite vos rustice gerere. Prae vos abdite dolorem vestrum, ut sinceram decet mulierem.

CARTESIUS

Helena, filiam meam videre cupio. Exquiratur filia mea ubicumque, in Francia, in Hollandia et vel in coloniis, si opus est. Francinam iubeo mihi adduci. (*He coughs.*) Antequam in tenebras mergar perpetuas, volo filiam meam quid sit lux docere. Mater mea asserere solebat semper prope me exstitisse, quotiescumque novas ratiocinationes haesitantibus verbis primo proferebam. Cum arbores nudae sunt foliis, oportet pulchras mulieres sibi circumdare. Propius accede, Helena, quaeso. (*Helena moves closer, mechanically.*)

HELENA

Filia nostra mortua est, ut bene nosti.

Quam crudelis es vindicta tua! En utique quod iram tuam vocas! Filiam meam deserere, hoc est ira tua. Nives cadunt, ut puto. Aestuo. (*speaking to Helena as if she were his servant*) Praebe mihi librum illum, illic super tabulam iacentem. Vellem, domine cardinalis, paginam quondam vobis ostendere. Exue vestem tuam, Helena. Te obsecro corpus tuum nudare, ut oculi mei quietem tandem inveniant. Fenestras pandite. (*Helena opens the window and shuts it immediately.*) Frigus est. Glacialis est algor iste. (*then, softly*) Quotiescumque frigore cursu vitae meae alsi, semper recordatus sum illius religiosae mulieris, iuvenis adhuc satis, in quam quondam Turonis incideram. Annus intercesserat ex nativitate Francinae. Adhuc bene memini. Glaciei fragmenta subgrundas obruerant. Grassa glacies agros undique operiebat. Aptis verbis religiosa illa delectabatur, verbisque utebatur ut magistra. Nihil aliud cogitabat nisi itinera. Nondum in monasterium intraverat, et iam nihil aliud desiderabat nisi longe profisci, in aliam terrae continentem. Quamvis vidua esset, de morte viri eius nullomondo commota videbatur. Filium habebat quem, ut asserebat, in optimas religiosasque manus relinquerat. Longius locuti eramus de vita et de corpore, praecipue tamen de passionibus animae. Passiones enim animae nos ubi nostra sistit sors perducunt. Illucescebat. Maria ad missam audiendam properabat. E coemeterio ego redibam, ubi de numero corporum quae suppeditari potuissent sciscitaveram, sperans utique mortuum quoddam corpus dissecari quantocius licere. Sperabam enim hac dissectione aliquid discere de illo 'igne sine luce' in nobis palpitante, tam fortiter interdum ut corpus nostrum calefaciat, quamvis animale sit et simplici machinae simile. Sitio. Aquam, aquam.

CARDINALIS

Citius aquam afferte homini isto. (*then, in a normal tone*) Propediem in Venetias et Romam iter arripiam.

Nolite, quaeso, nomina haec proferre urbium ubi tam felix et beatus fui. Sciatis deambulationes me semper amasse. Semper mihi gratum fuit secundum ripas Serenissimae perdiu deambulare, gaudium tamen maius accipiebam deambulando in Urbe, colles circumquaque ridentes oculis pervagando. Aquam, aquam!

Change of lighting. The atmosphere reverts to what it was when the four women first arrived, at the beginning of the chapter. The actresses stand around the bed like pallbearers arriving at and leaving a funeral. All are looking straight ahead.

NARRATOR

Why don't you give him something to drink?

CARLA

I can't. Not right now.

NARRATOR

He looks real.

CARLA

That's why I write novels. It seems real every time. And yet one is very afraid too.

NARRATOR

I don't like this passage of your book. It reminds me of Mother. I thought I had healed from the word *agony*. Is this passage really necessary?

CARLA

When a word troubles us, we must surround it with simple words that create images, like *Dutch tulips, Christmas tree* or *barrel organ*. In other circumstances, it's best to juggle words whose meanings are so ambiguous that they suck up part of our anxiety rather well.

You're right, Carla. All my life I've allowed myself to be taken, attracted, aroused by objects. When they rekindled overwhelming passions in me, I quickly turned them over so they'd show only the shape of their usefulness or their true worth on the artifacts market.

Walking by a lake has always been good for me – I mean it calms my mind. Blue, I've always had this fascination with blue. Simone, give me a bit of water. In the novel, Francine has beautiful blue eyes, a blue that could have healed the whole planet of all the sword thrusts and cannon fire that have ravaged the continents. It's because of war that we're sentenced to melancholy. (*Carla continues but now she's speaking on her own behalf.*) Walking by a lake like Mother used to do at fifteen, hair to the wind, a blade of grass and a story to tell between her lips. On her way to meeting herself and the summer to be, to have been.

My dear René, I don't much believe stories about melancholy. (*He seems to hesitate a moment.*) Oh! Maybe you're right after all. You know, if I put aside my soutane and my rank, I sink into some strange unknown that creates a sweet flavour under my tongue, with *je ne sais quoi* on my face that would remind me of my mother's hair whenever she leaned over to kiss my forehead. That's what you meant, right, that we all have a mother and a childhood?

(*indicating a character on a bed*)
Obviously she has no more energy.

It's not up to you to dictate my conduct.

Church bells are heard, as when people are leaving a funeral. Carla sits at the dressing table and starts removing her makeup.

I've seen writers dissolve into the multiplicity of possible frag-ments of life and fiction. They became incapable of choosing a subject. In fact, it was as if once literary creativity was democra-tized and globalized, writers no longer felt the need to choose. All subjects seemed to have the same value, the same flavour, could be used as entrails, garbage or makeup, suspended like little notches on the surfaces of sense and time. I've also known writers unable to take advantage of the silence available to them after loving or mourning. Toward the end I saw some who, in order to get noticed, put on airs – naïve, nerdy and inoffensive – so as not to frighten their readers or to have to make a statement about reality. On the contrary, in order to be noticed, women had to act violent, sexual and chock full of contradictions. Stuff it! Of course there were openings. The diversity of a barnyard always gets me dreaming. Rooster to donkey, dog to flea, cow to mouse. Yes, entering the wanderings of dogs, like getting to the heart of the matter by inventing dialogues for each species. Well, hey! I'm writing at a moment in history. Narrator, you're not saying a word, or maybe crumpled paper and paper balls no longer have a reason to exist because there are no more dele-tions, few erasures, and, if so, they're half-hearted. Every morn-ing in my room at the Clarendon, with its top-flight view of the St. Lawrence River, I dream of a generation that would be as concerned with silence as others are with sex – a silence come from cross-breeding the intelligences of all shapes of pain and pleasure that make us sigh, kneel down before the sea, force us to breathe it in until deep in the eye nothing else matters. Hey! Narrator, did you know that, right in front of my lassoed papa's house, I buried a Latin grammar book the Laramée sisters had entrusted me with like a treasure? Yes, in the same place where, lying on the cool ground, I invented playful scripts while thinking of Queen Christina and of the wide world slumbering inside me like a quiet volcano. And Narrator, did you know that one should always have or pretend to have a reader in mind when writing …

The narrator comes and stands in front of Carla, who thus disappears from view just as the whole scene goes to black. Curtain. Or

CHAPTER FIVE

I took notes up until the end without realizing the end had come. I wanted each moment to be whole, to let nothing escape me from the room or the set, from the face or the masks. I made careful note of the arrangement of the body, the placement of the furniture, the light outside and the lighting inside. In the next room, someone was listening to the same tango over and over again. It was hot. Nobody had thought of turning on the air conditioning or opening the window. Outside, the repeated sounds of heartbreaking church bells resonated. I was taking notes and somebody was dying amid the notes I was taking. We could have been in Madras, Petra, Québec City or Stockholm: somebody's soul was departing, wrapped in the fine tissue of what had been a love life. Slowly the paleness of dawn was leaving us, was depriving us of dreaming. For a period of time which seemed long, there was a constant to and fro, a strange ballet of doctors, interns, nurses, parents, discreet sweepers, extras, then figures and faces in the morning, which already was moving cunning grey and the yellow of eyedrops that blur vision and thinking.

I was right to want to stay behind to describe the objects while trying to slot them into time and history. Now I know there is a method for situating things in the adventure of cultures. Above all I know that the art of preservation is fully justified. Rings, watches, mirrors, masks or pens: every object conceals a story, a microscopic life which, when we discover it, breathes life back into the anonymous and absent-minded gestures with which we move and use objects. Perhaps we exist to name objects and perchance we do it in an erroneous way for the sheer pleasure of seeing a vase change into a rose and in its transparency enclose a beloved face, a novel landscape. Certainly objects are not quite things. For things have the power to move like events in a story: they happen, they die. Would that each one of my notices shed some light on objects, so that the thing inside them that draws them closer to us quivers and glitters with life.

I took notes until the end so as not to fall horizontally toward the summer to be. Before the end I would have liked to quit this obsession that binds me against my will to the idea that we mustn't be afraid to 'spit out' well-made well-said things about others. In the end, the woman I spent entire nights with, drinking and talking, never mentioned it, but that's what's at stake, regardless of what people say. Knowing how to spit out properly in language: contempt, anger, rebellion, joys, ecstasies and little hassles, desires and fits, while telling ourselves that all of this will surely strike the other at the most appropriate place in her humanity – there where, at every turn, hope and belief in the species can be recaptured.

Not for a moment did I lose sight of the bed, the body, the narrow mask that stuck to the skin of the face while, in a final effort, life did all it could to resemble nothing. Each batting of an eyelash, the slightest movement of the eyelids, the flooded dryness of the mouth, the wrong side of the scenery throbbing like an old screen at the very back of the pupils: all of this I made note of while thinking that I wanted to live with vast and unfurled thoughts so as to allow me always to brush against the vital energy generated by the sea over the centuries.

I would look into my mother's mouth. It was as if, by dint of looking there, I could transform the sun of dawn and that of dusk into felicitous twinklings – tiny silver shards which, in deflecting my attention, brought me, stage right, back to a misleading setting and a silence known to shelter verbs expressing time and a wealth of replies. Later on, I noted how the density of silence can vary, depending on whether it penetrates the mouth directly or if it carefully disperses the few words still living it up under tongue before night falls there forever.

I wrote, absorbed by my notes to the point of forgetting the city I was living in and the name of that woman I so enjoyed talking with. I copied out entire passages. It would no doubt have been possible for me to use other words to make my mother's face come back to life and to youth at the heart of the past, of its trends and music. But all those other words would have led me to lasso Mother in a life story. And all I wanted from life was movement. Not really stories. However, I made sure to note that the character of Carla Carlson had never been afraid of anything other than the obligation she'd created for herself to understand and simultaneously love the kind of noisy beat that generations transmit one to the other under the simple name of young life going its way.

One reply after another, I tackled the knots and bonds, seeking to understand how knots take shape starting from a word, around a hard self become complex or simply mysterious. Later on I did notice how the knots held a kind of softness and then, at the most unexpected moment, they'd loosen in spectacular fashion by installing characters, actors and witnesses around this soft part, all of them willing to startle anything that moves in cities and in dictionaries of proper names. I made note of how difficult it is to turn back or to pretend to be living innocently while holding the name of a woman, a character or a god between your teeth. All that time, someone was dying in front of me. Actresses with mascara tears facilitated the passage from reality to the nameless whiteness of elsewhere. I thought perfectly naked arms were needed for rapture, dreaming and agony which, along with its shadows, remains imprinted on the retina for a long time by striking at the very heart of our ability to imagine.

In the evening, back at the hotel, pockets full of bits of paper and matchbooks, I continued making note of low and high sounds, the soundless sentences that lodged at the back of my throat during the night and gave me sudden urges, like when we notice the softness with which early-morning light penetrates the drawn curtain or when it pours in as a single ray onto the pages of a well-written book left lying on the sofa.

By taking all these notes I thought I could go forth into the unspeakable, make existential loops with the memory I'd retained of the beauty of the sky and the city in the month of May. Attentive and alert in my every muscle until the very end, I did everything I could to be able to stand still in time so that life would result from life. The notes I took were like brief outings that allowed me to go and rummage through my mother's thoughts, to sweep into Simone Lambert's arms and to run between the pages written by Carla and the books I'd read during the last thirty years. I took notes because of the sea rustling in my head and of all things beautiful. More notes still to return to the idea of a *we*, of continuity under the sun.

I stayed in my room, moved by a seeker's passion no doubt inherited from my mother. While writing notes about the signs of the end, I became aware that I felt like leaving, going back outside to real life, indescribable because it seemed so minimalist yet at the same time so full of Rabelaisian curves. Curiously, this momentum drove me closer to reality, made me want to take it seriously, all the more so since I'd made a bet to enter its invisible part where, they say, life particles have no function other than to draw a curtain of illusions between us and the moment of our departure. Up, exhausted by the lack of sleep, I would think about the future of reality. Suddenly I'd see it as an exemplary science composed of laws and brainwaves that deserve to be explored every day with whys and explanations, a wealth of sighs and clandestine precautions.

Long after Mother's and Descartes's deaths, I kept on taking notes as if with every word I were digging a little tunnel into the word *universe*. That's where I wanted to go while looking at Mother's cheeks for the last time, Descartes's index finger pointed against his will, or so it seemed, toward the window and the snowy setting. Basically, all of this I did to get closer to the word *universe*, to fondle it, weigh it, cherish it like a certitude and a wound showing signs of healing.

Until the very end, despite tiredness and sleepiness, I sought to understand what had happened but without trying to reach a conclusion. I remain vigilant in the sole hope that nothing that was has been useless. Today I stand still facing the river. A book and a notebook under my arm, a rare pill in my Thai ring, a smile on my lips, I make note of everything that could pass for a story.

SOME NOTES

FOUND IN THE ROOM

AT THE HOTEL CLARENDON

I

A girl with large breasts is walking by the river. A Walkman at her waist, earphones plugged in, digital camera in her right hand, she stops every three metres to look at, pick up, put back a pebble coloured bone white, café au lait or jet black, while I think of the beach at Deauville, the cold wind that swept over mixed seafood platters whose names clatter in my ears. Another girl has come to sit on a bench protected by a wooden parasol. The girl has started to write in a large notebook, head down, her beautiful black hair falling over her cheeks. Ten metres of fine sand separate us like a big powder-blue barrel for trash, banana peels and apple cores. In front of us runs the river, today emerald green.

2

Language is made in such a way that one can jump upon its exceptions with both feet, crushing them with the full weight of our love and pain. *To burn* is a verb that suits me.

3

Make Carla say that she sometimes ponders what she calls *heavy identity*, a way of existing that removes all possibility of crashing into the lightness of being, or hitting it hard. She says also that we must know how to jump high in order to learn to fall on our past. She talks about the notion of *Tigersprung*, straight out of a Walter Benjamin metaphor. Tonight, I know the night will be a whiteout and that the black women inside us will be attentive to freedom and to the slightest whims of desire. Tonight, what happens will become real only once it's transcribed in the language we will have chosen. To discuss the forthcoming book and the violent energy at the utter edges of the body and its metaphors. Carla says metaphors serve to clear a path for the best intuitions slumbering inside us like living sunflowers or like those trees called flamboyants which, since she saw them in full bloom, have opened a door to ecstasy for her.

4

(Describe the stray dogs noticed yesterday morning on the Plains of Abraham. Leave the parenthesis open and flow into what follows:
as soon as night falls, Simone thinks about private life ...

5

roosters dogs dust without the commas.

6

we're always waiting for what comes next. As soon as a sentence begins, we're waiting for ...

7

sometimes she imagines herself drawing large Xs on the sea just like others who, with a single stroke, undo the landscape with a paintbrush, a machete, sink *a blade into the species* (save this expression for the title of a future book).

8

reality resists despite its air of innocence, its mad-cow speechlessness which, from afar, ends up looking like graffiti in the weary light of neons in the night

9

I miss Montréal. The smooth softness of the first
evenings in May when you can walk in the Old Port
breathing in the night with an idea of the unspeakable
in your throat. The urban din, the din of desire and of
its slow heat on the back of your neck, along the loins.
Blending aromas of tobaccos and the river.

10

Make Axelle speak more often. Give her desiring
energy. Create an effect. Make an effort of imagination. Use her desire as a lever for the future while also
questioning the autonomy of desire in relation to
trends, cultures and the language spoken. Look for
further information on what is known as *selfish DNA*.

11

Fear that reality might revert back to fiction in the
deepest dark of time. Fear of the opposite.

12

I think too often about pale Stockholm mornings, the
palm trees of Dublin. Observing others helps me live.
In the room next door, a chambermaid is singing
'La vie en rose.' Describe the streets of Québec and
Stockholm in greater detail.

Wound: n. (bef. 12c) injury to the body (as from violence,
accident or surgery) that involves laceration or break-
ing of a membrane (as the skin) and usu. damage to
underlying tissues.

    To wound ideas, decorum, modesty. Disappoint-
ment: today I find this word has a nameless blandness.

But yesterday I'd imagined it red like in the paintings of Caravaggio and Carpaccio. Or as an efficient metaphor falling like some slow dust imprinting the red of pain on our shoulders as in an Ann Hamilton installation.

Always pretend to be on the side of real life. Day of lightning and violent electricity. I accumulate notes, thoughts about ruins, the past. Yesterday, another terrible storm. During my museum visit, there was a blackout. Reread *The Passions of the Soul*.

I imagine her putting the page back into its context. Carla's hands are tanned, unadorned, with well-groomed nails. Calm hands which I'm unable to imagine on a computer keyboard. Hands that shape beautiful handwriting, supple, well adapted to the slowness of manuscript words. Fine skin under which the blood is fast-paced in the veins like a lively argument. Those hands make me travel through time. Carla's hands unbutton Hiljina's bodice. I foresee, I breathe in and I see her all over again.

Anxiety of words: animal vegetal little creature ara arab agreeable apple maple table saddle of rabbit rabid raccoon and harpoon ardent Harpagon, rage of Aragon, raccooning, cocooning, coconuts (nots) knot anew you open an ovum of colour and of cobra opera oeuvre hare snare and fare err and war jaw sigh slake the self and solo seem

Saw the stray dogs on the Plains of Abraham again. Five. Big mongrels, skinny and nervous, sniffing misery in the morning dew and the northern grass.

Continue the research on Francis Bacon's paintings, especially the series on screams produced in the fifties. Those screams he called *too abstract*. Screams which, when going through the mouth, transform the face into a terrifying gaping hole. Focus the research more specifically on the series of popes after Velázquez. Look carefully at the Velázquez painting entitled *Pope Innocent X* dated 1650, the year of Descartes's death.

Though highly moral, I do feel like I'm losing my ability to judge. Yesterday I took notes while a large black dog lay dying in front of me. Night of insomnia.

Try to retrace the sound work by Mark-Anthony Turnage, *Three Screaming Popes: after Francis Bacon for Large Orchestra*. Sixteen minutes.

Reread the unfinished manuscript again. There are days when, completely high on language, I really want a woman.

About theatre, make Carla say, 'People say that it's body. I say it's words in the present needing a tongue and muscles. Hence this curiosity I've developed about anatomy and the work of Mondino dei Liucci, and afterwards about the work of Descartes.'

Add: And then an image stands out from the others, outlined against the satiny ochre background of the bathroom. Alice is lying in the bathtub. Simone is kneeling on the white tile. She is scrubbing Alice's shoulders and back with a soap from Provence that multiplies the softness of the skin and of the gestures. Soap bubbles on the surface of the water, under her breasts, around her waist. Alice's skin is pink from the very hot water. Simone gazes into Alice's very soul, into that place where there is no more singular destiny. Alice kisses her. Simone holds up a dressing gown. Alice continues.

Stockholm in the black and white of dawn: a man walks bent over through the middle of the black ink of a print seen on Rue du Trésor before entering the Clarendon. Hubert Aquin walks the streets of a foreign city, staggering toward his fate. I can no longer keep holding up solitudes in the grey wind that whips the river.

We got into the habit of taking a walk on Dufferin Terrace. Sometimes she takes me by the arm like European women often do. It was hot yesterday; I could feel the softness of her skin, the warmth of her hand on my forearm. Today the river is violet. To look across to Lévis you have to shade your eyes, put your hand up horizontally, index finger against the forehead.

Black. In the course of her life Simone has been down into burial chambers, mausoleums, mastabas many a time. The fear of coming face to face with civilizations, cornered between their majestic silences and the terrifying echo of the screams sent into the cosmos by young and old women doomed since the dawn of time to circulate between the sand, the hands and the quartz of the hours.

The sorrow is huge. Don't know where it comes from, where it goes. At the movies it sometimes resurfaces when there's a separation, a departure. Huge sorrow that wedges in the throat, in the eyes, spreads through the chest like a burn, a suffocating embrace. I can't seem to understand the origins of this sorrow which belongs to no one in particular but circulates in our midst, contagious, exhausting and necessary like art that compels us to take care of what's most precious and vulnerable in us.

Have another look at the photographs taken by David McMillan during his six visits to Chernobyl and Pripet. Pictures of the unimaginable, or nostalgia-based photo evidence of our violent and sadistic brief passage through the forest and the seasons. McMillan quite probably wrote the captions for his photos himself. I like this one.

> *David McMillan*
> *Amusement Park, Pripet*
> *October 1994*
> *Chromogenic Print*
>
> *Pripet had most of the usual facilities of a modern Soviet city. The amusement park even had a Ferris wheel called 'the wheel of hell.' The accident happened just a few days before May 1st, a peak period of activity at the park. In this photo, the pale reddish glow of a meteor burning out as it falls from the sky is the only manifestation of movement.*

They say memory is ungovernable silence. So, all the better that writing makes it possible to redirect the course of things and to irrigate where the heart is dry and demanding.

It's just a little sentence for healing.

APPENDIX

Original text of pages 205 to 208. Please note that the Latin was intentionally not translated into classical Latin but rather into the vernacular Latin that could have been spoken by educated Europeans of the time. Specifically, the translator maintained (using certain syntactic structures typical of that Latin) the difference between the tu *(second person singular, akin to* ME thou: *singular, familiar) and the* vous *(second person plural, akin to* ME you/ye: *plural, respectful), unknown in classical Latin but of common usage in Medieval Latin.*

DESCARTES

What a strange room! I don't recognize it. What is that little curtain over there hiding, is it hiding the truth? Is it snowing? Helen, is it snowing? I can't seem to make out the fir tree, the very big, very tall tree that disturbs me every time my eyes come to rest on it as if it were a landscape unto itself. Helen, stay close to me. Give me your hand. Touch my forehead. Let me imagine you one last time. Naked. I would like you to be naked, one last time in front of my already failing eyesight. I would like to write again. I would like you to be naked. I want to write and you to be as naked as the dawn.

CARDINAL

Every time, however, we must let the shadow come close to us without chasing it away. Only the shadow makes agony genuine. There can be no version of agony without a shadow suspended above the lips that have loved their contemporaries and spoken well of the soul which we cannot see but which is there, which is there. We contain angers, my friend, which darken the summer light; I know whereof I speak, angers that don't subside as words go by, as ideas and reasoning go by.

HELEN

Oh! I know it all too well.

CARDINAL

I wasn't talking to you.

HELEN

(as if she hadn't heard)

Oh! I know it all too well. A fit of anger is a deep pain that one day violently lodges itself in our limbs wild with despair. Once settled in our nervous system, it can only weaken us, deceive our senses and our desires. René, you've no idea of my anger. I strain to conceal its source from you every single day, as well as the horrid twitching of the hands and eyelids it provokes. Today I've had enough. I'm speaking up.

CARDINAL

Don't be vulgar. Keep your pain to yourself like a real woman should.

DESCARTES

Helen, I want to see my daughter. Search for my daughter wherever she may be, in France, in Holland, all the way to the colonies if need be; I order (*he coughs*) that Francine be brought to me. I want to instruct my daughter about the nature of light before I fade away forever. Mother always said she'd been there by my side when I stammered out a new line of reasoning. When the trees are bare, one must be surrounded by pretty women. Helen, I beg you, come a bit closer. (*Helen approaches mechanically.*)

HELEN

You know very well our daughter is dead.

DESCARTES

How cruel your revenge is! This is what you call your anger! This is your anger. Abandoning my daughter. It's snowing, isn't it? I'm hot. (*talking to Helen as if she were his servant*) Give me that book over there on the table. There's a passage, Cardinal, that I want to show you. Undress, Helen, I beg you to undress so that my eyes can rest at last. Open the window. (*Helen opens the window for a moment then quickly shuts it.*) It's cold. Freezing cold. (*then, softly*) Every time I've been cold in my life, I thought about that young nun I met in Tours. It was a year after Francine's birth. I remember. There were icicles hanging from the gutters. The fields were covered with a thick sheet of ice. The nun loved words and used them like a master. All she did was dream of travelling. She had just entered the convent and already all she could think about was going far away, to another continent. Even though she was a widow, she didn't seem at all affected by her husband's death. She had a son whom she said she'd left in capable religious hands. We talked at length about life and the body. Of the soul's passions more especially, for they are the ones that lead us to our destiny. The day was dawning, Marie was going to mass. I was returning from the cemetery where I'd inquired about the number of corpses available, hoping a dissection would soon be possible so that I could finally further my knowledge about the 'fire without light' that sometimes pulses so loudly inside us that it heats our body, which is both animal and simple machine. I'm thirsty. Water! Water!

CARDINAL

Bring this man something to drink, quickly. (*then, in a normal tone*) I'm leaving for Venice and Rome soon.

DESCARTES

Oh! I beg you, don't utter the names of those cities where I was so happy. I am a lover of long walks, you know. Taking long walks along the canals of La Serenissima was a great joy for me, though I confess not as great as what I experienced walking through Rome, looking at its joyful hills curving the horizon. Water! Water!

The quotation from the Homero Aridjis poem on page 171 was excerpted from 'Ojos de otro mirar'/'Eyes to See Otherwise,' *A White Body in the Desert*, trans. George McWhirter (New York: New Directions, 2001).

How much has the eye to weigh in the balance?
What does the dream between two eyelids measure?
How much does a closed eye, the eye of death,
an eye peeled weigh in your hand?

Also featured in this novel are quotes from Assia Djébar, Silvina Ocampo, Violette Leduc and Dante Alighieri.

3

Our Lady of the Flowers by Jean Genet

To the Lighthouse by Virginia Woolf

Paradiso by José Lezama Lima

L'obéissance by Suzanne Jacob

Benito Cereno by Herman Melville

Le monde sur le flanc de la truite by Robert Lalonde

The Euguelion by Louky Bersianik

Running in the Family by Michael Ondaatje

The Book of Promethea by Hélène Cixous

Heroine by Gail Scott

Childhood by Nathalie Sarraute

Tomorrow in the Battle Think on Me by Xavier Marias

Molloy by Samuel Beckett

Crossing the River by Caryl Phillips

The Last of the African Kings by Maryse Condé

Time Regained by Marcel Proust

The First Man by Albert Camus

Fortuny by Pere Gimferrer

The Little Girl Who Was Too Fond of Matches by Gaétan Soucy

Death of Virgil by Hermann Broch

Fontainebleau by Michael Delisle

Le soir du dinosaure by Cristina Peri Rossi

Blue Eyes, Black Hair by Marguerite Duras

Un homme est une valse by Pauline Harvey

My Year in the No-Man's-Bay by Peter Handke

Les derniers jours de Noah Eisenbaum by Andrée Michaud

Pereira Declares by Antonio Tabucchi

Two Stories of Prague by Rainer Maria Rilke

Next Episode by Hubert Aquin

Cobra by Severo Sarduy

La vie en prose by Yolande Villemaire

The Lesbian Body by Monique Wittig

Technique du marbre by Béatrice Leca

Mauve Desert by Nicole Brossard

Extinction by Thomas Bernhard

The Opposing Shore by Julien Gracq

Thérèse and Isabelle by Violette Leduc

La déconvenue by Louise Cotnoir

Meroë by Olivier Rolin

These Festive Nights by Marie-Claire Blais

In the Shadow of the Wind by Anne Hébert

The Christmas Oratorio by Goran Tunstrom

Le livre du devoir by Normand de Bellefeuille

Nightwood by Djuna Barnes

The Tin Flute by Gabrielle Roy

E. Luminata by Diamela Eltit

The Palace by Claude Simon

Parc univers by Hugues Corriveau

The Sea by Michelet

Microcosms by Claudio Magris

Dios No Nos Quiere Contentos by Griselda Gambaro

La nuit by Jacques Ferron

The Heart Is a Lonely Hunter by Carson McCullers

The Swallower Swallowed by Réjean Ducharme

Paulina 1880 by Pierre-Jean Jouve

Memoria by Louise Dupré

Dust over the City by André Langevin

Pylon by William Faulkner

A Universal History of Infamy by Jorge Luis Borges

The Autobiography of Alice B. Toklas by Gertrude Stein

Jos Connaissant by Victor-Lévy Beaulieu

The Life and Opinions of Tristram Shandy, Gentleman by Laurence Sterne

Nous parlerons comme on écrit by France Théoret

Life: A User's Manual by Georges Perec

About the Author

Born in Montréal, poet, novelist and essayist NICOLE BROSSARD has published more than thirty books since 1965 and has twice won the Governor General's Award for her poetry. Many of her books have been translated into English: *Mauve Desert, The Aerial Letter, Picture Theory, Lovhers, Baroque at Dawn, The Blue Books, Installations, Museum of Bone and Water* and, more recently, *Intimate Journal*. She has co-founded and co-directed the literary magazine *La Barre du Jour* (1965–1975), has co-directed the film *Some American Feminists* (1976) and co-edited the much acclaimed *Anthologie de la poésie des femmes au Québec*, first published in 1991 and then in 2003. She has also won le Grand Prix de Poésie du Festival International de Trois-Rivières in 1989 and 1999. In 1991, she was awarded le Prix Athanase-David (the highest literary recognition in Québec). She is a member of l'Académie des lettres du Québec. She won the 2003 W. O. Mitchell Prize. Her work has been widely translated into English and Spanish and is also available in German, Italian, Japanese, Slovenian, Romanian, Catalan and other languages. Nicole Brossard writes and lives in Montréal.

About the Translator

SUSANNE DE LOTBINIÈRE-HARWOOD lives and teaches in Montréal, her hometown. She is the author of *Re-belle et infidèle: la traduction comme pratique de ré-écriture au féminin / The Body Bilingual: translation as a rewriting in the feminine* (Remue-ménage/Women's Press, 1991), and of many texts about her practice of both literary and art-text translation. As a translator she has co-authored numerous works of theory and fiction into English and into French. Her practice has led to parallel art experiences such as years of 'performative lecturing' in North America and Europe, and an exhibition of her art-text translation artifacts (La Centrale/ Powerhouse, Montréal, 2001). This is the third Nicole Brossard novel she has translated (the other two are *Mauve Desert* and *She Would Be the First Sentence of My Next Novel*).

Typeset in Granjon
Printed and bound at the Coach House on bpNichol Lane, 2005

Translated by Susanne de Lotbinière-Harwood
Edited and designed by Alana Wilcox
Cover design by Stan Bevington
Cover image, *In that inner space*, by Betty Goodwin [1994, Graphite and oil
    stick over gelatin silver print on translucent mylar film (Cronaflex),
    94 by 73.6 cm]. Courtesy of the Galerie René Blouin, Montreal.

Coach House Books
401 Huron St. (rear) on bpNichol Lane
Toronto, Ontario
M5S 2G5

1 800 367 6360
416 979 2217

mail@chbooks.com
www.chbooks.com